Also by Torrey Maldonado

TIGHT
SECRET SATURDAYS

TORREY MALDONADO

 Nancy Paulsen Books

NANCY PAULSEN BOOKS
An imprint of Penguin Random House LLC, New York

Copyright © 2020 by Torrey Maldonado
Penguin supports copyright. Copyright fuels creativity, encourages diverse voices,
promotes free speech, and creates a vibrant culture. Thank you for buying an authorized
edition of this book and for complying with copyright laws by not reproducing, scanning,
or distributing any part of it in any form without permission. You are supporting writers
and allowing Penguin to continue to publish books for every reader.

Nancy Paulsen Books is a trademark of Penguin Random House LLC.

Visit us online at penguinrandomhouse.com

Library of Congress Cataloging-in-Publication Data
Names: Maldonado, Torrey, author.
Title: What lane? / Torrey Maldonado.
Description: New York: Nancy Paulsen Books, [2020] | Summary: Biracial
sixth-grader Stephen questions the limitations society puts on him after he
notices the way strangers treat him when he hangs out with his white
friends and learns about the Black Lives Matter movement.
Identifiers: LCCN 2019043556 | ISBN 9780525518433 (hardback)
ISBN 9780525518440 (ebook)
Subjects: CYAC: Racism—Fiction. | Friendship—Fiction.
Black lives matter movement—Fiction. | Racially mixed people—Fiction.
African Americans—Fiction. | Brooklyn (New York, N.Y.)—Fiction.
Classification: LCC PZ7.M2927 Wh 2020 | DDC [Fic]—dc23
LC record available at https://lccn.loc.gov/2019043556

Printed in the United States of America
ISBN 9780525518433

1 3 5 7 9 10 8 6 4 2

Design by Suki Boynton
Text set in Berling LT Std

For Ava.
The world is yours.

CHAPTER 1

"THIS MOVIE IS lit." Dan aims his TV remote to start *Spider-Man: Into the Spider-Verse*. "Chad *hated* it. I played it for him here. All he said was 'Trash. They shoulda kept Spider-Man white.'"

"What?!" I shake my head. "He's wack. How you both even cousins?"

He lowers the remote. "He's not wack."

My parents' voices in my head say, *Blood is thicker than water*. Family picks family over friends.

I ease up and stare at the window.

Chad is Dan's cousin, and he just moved to our neighborhood. He's a sixth grader like us. So far, I'm not feeling him. Anything I say, he contradicts. Anytime I'm around, he puts me down.

I hate how Dan doesn't notice and now even defends him.

Me and Dan live in connecting buildings and we're over at each other's so much, we practically live in the same apartment. And we're both into superheroes, fantasy, sci-fi, and similar stuff. Basically, we're twins, except we look opposite. He's white-white. I'm not. People sometimes call me Stephen Curry from basketball because of our names, skin color, and features. We even fade our fros similar.

"So, Stephen, not only is this new Spider-Man almost our age, it gets better. He's from Brooklyn too. His full name is Miles Morales, he's fourteen, and—"

I'm amped again. "Skip explaining. *Show* me."

"Just so you know, the movie is kinda violent, so don't get scared."

"Dan, you funny. You know all movies are my lane."

"Nah! You run if people get hurt or bloody."

"Run?! *When?*"

He sits next to me and poses like me watching TV. "This wasn't you? When we saw *Stranger Things?*" His leg gets jumpy and he changes his voice into mine: "I'ma get ice cream. You want?"

"What?! I didn't do that."

"Yeah. You. Did."

I stare from him to my wrist, at the only bracelet I rock. It's black with bright white glow-in-the-dark letters that say WHAT LANE?

Last year, I got it on a school trip to a Barclays Center basketball game. There, this player Marshall Carter, nicknamed MC, was on that *next* next level. He kept scoring—*any* way he wanted. Everyone else had a lane. They had sick passes or swished in half-court shots. Marshall was wavy in *every* lane. He bagged three-pointers, passed like *whoa*, and did crossovers that made guys fall on their butts. And almost every time he scored, he'd yell, "What lane?!" and WHAT LANE? flashed on the JumboTron. He had *no* lane.

That day, I bought MC's bracelet after the game. I wanted his saying on my arm. *What lane?!*

I want to be that: in every lane, have no lane.

Now I thumb my bracelet. "Dan, this movie is my lane too. Press Play."

Dan aims his remote at the screen, and when it starts, we point. "Times Square!"

Then we shout again: "Empire State Building!"

New York City spots at night keep flashing. This. Is. So. Tight! I love when my city gets to shine.

At one point, he elbows me. "How wild is it that Miles can pass for you or your brother, if you had one?"

"Facts." Miles Morales could be *me*. He's half African American too, and even though his other side is Puerto Rican and mine is white, most people say we Black.

I can't believe Chad called this movie trash. Me and Dan are *into it*–into it.

Most movies have superheroes who match Dan and Chad: Captain America, Superman, Thor, the Flash, and more.

It's wavy that *this* Spider-Man looks like half of my family.

We're all the way into a scene when we hear Dan's dad shout, "Dan!"

Dan rolls his eyes. "Try to ignore him. This movie is whoa, right?"

"Yeah. It stays this good?"

"Whaaaaat?! It gets *way* better."

"DANIEL!" his dad yells now. "Didn't you hear me? It's time for Stephen to go. And time for you to take out the trash. *Now.*"

"Ugh!" Dan shuts off the TV and we bounce.

CHAPTER 2

THE TRASH DUMPSTER is in front of an alley in between me and Dan's buildings. Sometimes, shady guys who don't live here dip in and out of the alley. The only time me and Dan ever went past the dumpster was when our old super, who took care of our buildings, let us check out the Halloween decorations he kept in the basement. He was cool. This new super? Nah. He's not. He eyes me funny.

Dan spots something. "You see the top of the ramp?"

I check the ramp attached to his building. "The mask?"

"Yeah. Scary eyes, right?"

I kinda wish I wasn't seeing this scary werewolf mask. Its lips growl back real angry, showing long bloody fangs, and its cheek is torn open, half-eaten. But it's more than that—it's how the mask sits on top of a mop that leans against the wall that makes it scarier. It reminds me of a vampire movie trailer that showed these human heads stuck on poles like trophies.

Sometimes horror trailers pop up on the screen with no warning and I see things I wish I could forget. Then I end up with nightmares.

Dan says, "I wonder if the new super is getting out Halloween decorations for our lobbies."

That makes sense. It's almost Halloween.

Dan squints. "Hold up."

"What?"

"Look *down* the ramp."

The metal door at the bottom is propped open with a brick. Usually it's locked.

Dan's curious. "You think he's down there?"

I shrug.

"C'mon," he says. "Let's check. Maybe he'll let us mess with Halloween stuff like the last super."

"Nah, this super's not that way," I say. "And what if we run into a shady head who . . . ?"

Dan ignores me, flops his trash into the dumpster, and turns and tiptoes into the alley.

I watch him. I can't let him go solo—he's my boy. I follow.

Dan nods at me. "You ready, Miles?"

Him calling me Spider-Man amps me up. Miles'd go down this alley, easy. Yeah, I got this.

From the top of the ramp, the door is an open mouth—grinning us in, or waiting to swallow us.

"What you think?" he asks. "Anyone down there?"

I grab his forearm. "Hold up."

In this sci-fi show I saw, a girl did something smart. She stood at a doorway and threw something into a room to see if the monster hiding would jump out.

I grab a baseball-size rock off the floor and pitch it.

CLANG! My rock clanks off the metal door.

Dan's confused. "Why you throw that fo—?"

"If someone's in there, we'll know. They'll come out."

He watches the door. "Oh. Smart."

No one comes out.

I smile. "We good."

We slowly creep down the ramp and don't even get halfway when a guy pedaling fast-fast on a mountain bike flies past us.

Top speed, me and Dan sprint up the ramp and back outside, where Junior, our new super, shouts from where he's fixing a window up on the fire escape. He's mad, waving his fist at the biker. *"Come back here! Thief!"*

Then he yells at us. No. *At me.* "That boy your friend?"

Dan is SOS—Stuck On Stupid. So am I.

Huh? Junior's asking if he's *my* friend?

Dan yells up at the fire escape, "No! We don't know him. What happened?"

"Ay! That's my bike! I keep it down there. He took it!" Junior waves Dan off and points at me. "YOU! *You* know that boy!"

He's not asking. He's saying.

"Wha—?!" I'm shocked. "No! Why would I know h—?"

Junior interrupts me. "You told your friend to take it?"

Just then, three things hit me. First, Junior is for real and swears I know that bike thief. Second, he automatically feels Dan is innocent. Then, as I realize the third thing, it comes out my mouth. "Because we're Black."

Dan hears me. "What?"

"Dude. Junior thinks me and that bike thief are tight since we both Black."

"Nah. I don't think so."

Junior's eyes now laser in on me and he starts cursing in Spanish.

Dan yells up at Junior, "Don't be mad at us. Be mad at you! This is your fault! If you locked up your bike, you'd have one!"

"C'mon." I tap Dan. "Forget him."

As we pass the trash dumpster, he fist-bumps me so we can split into our separate buildings.

But before he leaves, Dan says, "Stephen. Junior was foul. Like we did something bad."

In my head, I think, *No, not we. He was foul like I did something bad.*

CHAPTER **3**

THE NEXT DAY after school, me and Dan meet outside our buildings and head to the park a few blocks from us. Our friends usually chill on the picnic tables between the track and handball courts.

Normally, we go straight there, but Dan stops me as we pass the little stone shack in the park with the Parks Department leaf logo on it.

"Stephen." He points at the open door, then at the Parks Department workers near their truck on the other side of the park. "This *has* to be empty. The workers are way over there."

"Dude." I roll my eyes up at the sky. "Remember yesterday? Junior?"

"Stephen, c'mon. It won't be yesterday. No Juniors are here to yell at us."

I cut on him. "What's up with you and doors? You Alice in Wonderland or something? Can't we just go from A to B?"

"B for Boring? Let's *do this*."

I want to say no, but sometimes I'm like my dad. He says yes to people a lot just to make them happy or shut them up.

Dan inches toward the shack and pokes his head in. "They listen to rap."

I peek in. The workers' radio plays on a shelf next to some cleaning supplies. Mops and brooms stand nearby that. Workers' uniforms are on hangers.

"Remember you said B is for Boring?" I ask. "This is that. Let's dip."

"No," Dan says. "The fun is *going in*. C'mon. Or you're scared?"

I thumb my bracelet's letters: WHAT LANE? I stare at the Parks Department workers, so far-off I can pinch them between my fingers. I scan everyone else chilling outside. No one pays us mind. "A'ight, whatevs."

Me and Dan step into the middle of the room. I'm nervous but good. He turns up the radio's volume and gets me all jumpy.

"For real?" My eyes pop. "You want people hearing this and coming in?"

Dan pulls a uniform shirt off a hanger. "Wanna try this on?"

"Nah, bruh. You. Bump that. Hang it up. You just acting dumb now."

Dan hangs it back up, and I lower the radio and peek outside. "The workers are still far. Let's bounce."

Dan follows me out. I feel a few things. My heart knocks hard and fast in my chest, but I also feel good for shutting him down. Since I was little, it's been hard to speak up. In classes, lots of kids spoke up like no biggie, but it was hard for me.

I was that way all the way up to age nine on New Year's, when I first learned what a New Year's resolution is. Something you plan to do. Right there, I told myself, *From now on, I'll say what's on my mind.*

I didn't always keep that promise, but I got better. Like just now. I kept that New Year's resolution: I spoke my mind.

⇆

We get to the picnic benches, and our friends Christopher, Jen, and Jeremiah are there with a bunch of other kids.

Dan gets braggy as we get close. "Guess what we did. Snuck in that shack."

Everyone looks like, *Nuh-uh*. Then they're all questions.

Jen: "What's in there?"

Christopher: "For how long?"

Jeremiah: "Swear?"

Then Dan's cousin Chad skateboards here from nowhere. His clothes are ripped as usual. He has a rep for climbing and trespassing into places.

He obviously heard what me and Dan just did in that Parks Department shack, because he smirks at me. "What's up, *Stranger Things*?" He points at my *Twilight Zone* T-shirt. "Did you enter another dimension? See 'spirits'?"

Ugh. Here he goes again, calling me names and leaning on "spirits" like a dis.

I eye Dan to see if he gets it about Chad, but Dan seems clueless.

"Hey." Chad points at an abandoned factory rising high in the distance like the Tower of Terror at Disney. "The construction company is blowing up that old building. I heard back in the day, some workers died in a fire there. You guys want to see *real* spirits? Go in *there* with me. Bet spirits—ghosts, whatever you call them—are in there."

I think about what it must be like in there. Maybe like *Ghost Hunters*? Do I even want to see that stuff in real life? I get a *Nah* feeling, but everyone else starts fist-bumping Chad.

Jen says, "That's kinda next-level! I've never snuck into an abandoned building before." She's cool, a tough girl who does parkour and our school's martial arts program. I've held boards she's punched in half.

Her twin brother, Jeremiah, flicks back his long rock-star-looking hair that matches Jen's. "I bet inside'll feel haunted. Real Halloweeny."

"Yeah." Chad turns to me. "A kind of haunted house. You down?"

Dang. Why's he putting it on me?

As everyone eyes me, all I can think to say is "Yeah, I'm down."

I think of my dad, agreeing with people to make them happy, or to shut them up. It works for my dad and it works right now.

I wish I wasn't that little me who struggles to speak up again.

CHAPTER **4**

OUTSIDE THIS SCARY factory's fence, I check for people and see only an old man pushing a shopping cart. Behind him is a cemetery.

This is kray. Sneaking in a haunted-looking factory. Next to a cemetery.

Everyone eyes for a way through the fence.

Jeremiah nods at the fence's top. "Barbed wire. I'm not going over that."

Everyone's looking everywhere but down—which is where I see a way we might get in. And beyond that, I stare through the fence at the broke-down-looking door on the factory, where a locked chain sags. *I bet we can squeeze through that door.* I shake off the thought, because then what? We're in a scary scene from *Ghost Hunters?*

Then Chad shocks us by jumping on the fence and climbing up, *fast.*

One by one, kids remind him.

"You'll get hurt!"

"There's barbed wire!"

"Watch out!"

Chad pauses, stares down at us like he's Batman or someone. The soles of his kicks are a foot above our heads. "There has to be a way around the wire." He goes back to climbing.

"Chad!" Dan yells up to him. He points down the block. "Cops!"

Chad freezes. The only way he'll make it down is if—

He jumps.

CRASH! Landing on two feet, he crumples on the ground.

For a split second he lies there and I feel grimy. I could've pointed the way in under the fence . . .

But then he stands, brushing himself off. "Act normal when the police pass."

We all pretend to talk and laugh as the cop car cruises closer.

Suddenly, a thought comes to mind: *Everyone here is all white except me.*

"Stephen," Jen says on the low to me. "You're laughing fake. Laugh *normal.*"

The cop car gets close and the white bald-shaven cop who's driving squints at me. *Is he eyeing me different than how he's looking at everyone else?*

Dan waves at the cop. "Hi," he yells. "Nice day, huh?"

Sergeant Baldie's eyes slide to Dan, and he gives him a nod back.

As soon as the cop car turns, we all walk *fast* from the construction site, but I walk fastest.

Chad cracks on me. "You nervous or something?"

When we exit the park, we split in different directions. Except Chad. He stays with me and Dan. Ugh. Why couldn't he have bounced too?

I wish Chad didn't live four blocks from us now.

Better yet, I wish he'd moved to another planet.

CHAPTER 5

"SEE THIS?" CHAD wants us to look at his phone.

"What?" Dan crowds him. I hesitate, then check his phone too.

Chad points at a YouTube video of a Black man on a stage. "You know this comedian?"

We shake our heads no.

He keeps on. "Watch him joke about how Black people act when craziness happens outside."

I'm confused. *Why's Chad bringing this up? And Black jokes? He's white.*

The comedian acts it out. "If something strange happens outside, white people act like this . . ." He makes his voice extra white and nasally and starts walking all concerned. "'What's happening over here? We should investigate.'" The comedian laughs. "White people walk right into the craziness! But Black people? We do this." He switches into a hood Black voice, pretends to be in the middle of a conversation, spots another Black person running from whatever, then *sprints* across the stage.

Chad lets out a laugh *so hard.* "Oh man, that's so true."

Dan chuckles.

It's legit funny to them.

To me? Maybe it'd be funny if it wasn't Chad showing it. It doesn't feel funny because they're laughing at me. I smirk.

"Yesterday, Stephen, you ran that way from the super," Dan says.

"He did?" Chad asks, too thirsty to know more.

I shake my head. "Nah, Dan—we *both* ran that way."

"But you zoomed off like the Flash. I couldn't keep up."

"You just hating 'cause I'm faster than you."

Chad's watches us beef, loving it.

Why do I feel ganged up on all of a sudden? Because they're cousins? Because they're both white? Sandwiching me over some joke about me and Black people?

I get serious. "Wait, Dan. You say I ran like that because my dad is Black? And, you, Chad, show me this video because you racist?"

Dan's jaw drops. He holds up his open hands like *Whoa!* and starts apologizing. "I didn't mean anything by it. I wasn't trying to be racist."

But Chad doesn't deny he's acting all racist.

"This video is wack," I say, and then try to change the subject. "You know what's tight, though? It's Halloween soon." I point to a shop's window full of costumes.

"For real," Dan says. "It *is* October first today."

"I wonder if they sell a Miles Morales costume. They'd make bank. So many kids will want to be Miles. I'm gonna see if they have him and other Black heroes."

"What Black heroes you mean? There's just Miles Morales. Oh, and Black Panther." Chad talks like some cocky expert who's glad there's almost *no* Black heroes.

"Nah, there's more. Not *enough* Black superheroes, but more than Miles and Black Panther. Dan, let's take turns naming some until we can't."

Dan jumps in. "Luke Cage!"

"Cyborg from *Teen Titans* and *Justice League*."

"War Machine from *Iron Man*."

I put my fist over my heart. "My bae. Storm from *X-Men*."

Dan shakes his head. "Your bae! Whatevs. Anyway, that Black Green Lantern."

We go back and forth more, and either Chad's not into this game or he's not feeling Black superheroes.

"I'm out." He fist-bumps Dan and skates off.

No fist bump for me. Not even a nod.

I watch Chad roll away. The past two days have gotten me tight. Something says tell Dan why. "That video was annoying. It kinda proved I *should* run since I'm Black."

"What?" Dan gets dead serious. "Why?"

"C'mon. You saw what happened yesterday, with Junior swearing I knew that bike thief just because we're Black. Maybe the video is saying Black people stand out and we're targets for people to think we in the wrong when we not. So we should run and not get in trouble for nothing."

"Nah."

"C'mon. Today isn't more proof of that? Did you see the cop at the factory eye me differently than everyone?"

"I didn't. And why would he do that?"

"Because everyone was white. And I'm not."

"That's not true. Everyone wasn't white."

"Everyone wasn't white?"

"No . . ." He bites his lip. "What about . . ." It hits him. "Bruh . . . you're *right*. I never thought about that before."

I stare at him, wondering how he hasn't. But

then again, he's not the one people act prejudiced toward.

Then a thought hits me. *Are we in two different lanes?* I get seen as trouble but he gets left alone?

I hate thinking that.

Dan interrupts the awkward quiet. "I'm sorry."

"Sorry for what?"

He shrugs. "I don't know. Maybe I should notice stuff more. What you notice."

And wow. Wowwowwow. It feels so good hearing Dan say that.

"Word." I put up my fist and he fist-bumps me back.

CHAPTER **6**

A FEW DAYS later, I wait outside the supermarket while Dan dips in to get stuff for his mom.

My neighborhood is cool for people-watching. Right now, a college-aged guy who looks mixed like me *flies* down the street on one of those expensive electronic skateboards with just one wheel in the middle. He swerves to avoid hitting a skinny white guy with a beard standing at the bus stop.

"Watch yourself!" The skinny bearded guy has to jump out the way.

He's one of lots of young white guys on this street who my parents joke about and call *beardos*. I see how many I can spot.

Right now, one's walking by with a woman carrying a yoga mat. A beardo in sandals walks his dog, and another pushes a baby stroller. One comes out of the corner café with a tray full of cups.

Me and my dad went into that café once, and when we saw that the smallest-size coffee cost five dollars, we never went back. Nowadays our neighborhood has lots of these expensive cafés.

A cop car parks near the bus stop and two white male cops get out.

All of a sudden, I want to try to do what Dan did outside the factory. So when one cop makes eye contact with me, I wave and say hi.

The cop's stare asks, *You talking to me?* He elbows his partner and nods in my direction. His partner shrugs.

Okaaaay, I think. *No friendly nods. That did NOT work for me the way it worked for Dan.*

Maybe their stares mean nothing. Maybe they're just trying to figure me out. But they could've at least said hi back. I feel uncomfortable now, so I go in the supermarket.

I'm up and down aisles until I finally spot Dan at this cookie display in the bakery section. He's at one of those glass displays where you bag the cookies you want.

He opens the case, takes a cookie, and starts chewing.

I walk up on him. "Stop." I thumb at the white man stacking a display who eyes him. "Dan, don't you need to pay first?"

He just keeps chewing. "My parents do this. They sample stuff to see if they want to buy it."

The way he chews makes this cookie look extra good!

I check back, and that man has no reaction.

I guess it's fine to sample.

I bite. "Dang. This is goo—"

The white man is up on me. "Excuse me. Did you pay for that?"

My jaw drops.

How's he only talking to me? Dan is right here chewing too. "I'm . . . we're just sampling this."

That man eyes *me* like I'm a criminal.

"Come with me. You have to pay for that."

He starts walking me toward the registers and talks real loud and braggy to a nearby white co-worker. "This boy tried to steal a cookie. I'm making him pay for it."

I'm embarrassed. I feel powerless. And I can't believe he just left Dan there, eating a cookie.

Then Dan catches up to us. "Mister, what are you doing? Don't you see me? I was right there, eating a cookie too."

This man stares at Dan like Dan speaks a foreign language. "What?"

"Why didn't you stop me like you stopped my friend?"

"This is your friend?"

"Yeah!"

"How do I know you ate a cookie?" the man says. "He has one in his hand. You don't."

Dan opens his mouth. Cookie mush is still on his tongue. "See?"

The man is SOS.

Dan says, "If you let me go, you gotta let him go." Then he speaks in the same tone as when he yelled at Junior to leave us alone. "Or if he's in trouble, I should be too!"

The man waves Dan off. "Okay, take your friend. Both of you go home and don't come back to the bakery. This is *my* department."

It feels like the whole supermarket's looking at us now, and I feel lower than dirt.

Dan acts the opposite. He might as well be the boss here. "I'll leave *after* I get what I came for." He shakes his head. "Like this is *your* aisle. Like you *own* the store."

"It *is* my aisle." The man points to his shirt label that says **BAKED GOODS**.

Dan waves him off. "Free country."

I'm telling you. I would *neeeeeeeever* talk to a grown man that way. I whisper to Dan, "Let's just bounce."

He walks back into the aisle and snatches something off the shelves from his mom's list before we head to the register.

⇆

Outside the supermarket, we wait at the corner for the light to let us walk.

"I noticed," Dan says.

I'm still in my head replaying what happened in the store. "What?"

"What you said. About being Black. About sticking out. Being a target. I noticed."

I nod, feeling what happened in that store was so foul.

Dan looks back at the supermarket, then at me. "I know that's why that man did that. You want me to tell someone he did that? My parents?"

I look past Dan at the supermarket. Then back at him. "Nah. It's dead."

Dan had my back in there. He didn't have to, but he stepped up for the same punishment as me. He's always been my boy with a lot of things. It's cool he was my boy with this too.

CHAPTER **7**

JUST FROM MY face, my parents can tell when I'm upset. They've been reading me since forever, so I'm glad only my dad is home.

Just one parent to avoid.

But my pops maybe catches me trying to dodge him.

I head to the kitchen, and he's following a few feet behind me.

I go to my bedroom. He's still shadowing me.

Everywhere I go, he goes.

This could be an ill game of tag, except now it's not fun.

I sit on the floor and pretend he's not standing at my door. I soft-pitch my handball with the New York Yankees logo on it at the wall and catch it over and over, avoiding eye contact.

My dad's reflexes are mad fast—his nickname when he was little was Speedy, since he was so quick in sports. So when he snatches my handball in mid-air as it flies fast to the wall, my eyes flick at him on instinct because his speed is whoa.

Our eyes lock and it's a wrap.

"What's wrong?" he asks.

I mutter about that white guy.

Dad sits on my bed. "Keep on."

I tell him the full. He nods over and over, spinning the handball in his fingers nonstop.

When I'm done, he says, "I'm not blaming you. You didn't do anything wrong. But what made you take that cookie?"

"I saw Dan do it. Except he got a different reaction." I pause. I want to tell my dad more—that over the last few days, lots of different people've been prejudiced with me. But how can I tell him about the white cop eyeing me at the factory without letting him know we tried to trespass? And I don't want him starting anything with Junior. So instead, I ask, "Dad, why is racist stuff happening to me all of a sudden? I mean, in elementary it wasn't like this. *So much*, you know?"

"You shot up. You're not a little boy anymore. People outside are starting to see you differently." Dad sighs. "And a lot of white people see boys with your height and they don't see your age. They see what they imagine or what the media teaches them to think about Black men—maybe that we're threats or troublemakers. You want to hear of something similar that happened to me?"

I pull my desk chair right in front of him and sit. "Go."

"Do you want something from when I was in elementary? Middle school? High school? College? Or when I was getting my master's? Maybe this week where I teach?"

I don't believe him. *Where he teaches?!*

He's the man at his high school. I know; I visited him there. I can't see anyone there making him feel weak or wack.

I tell him, "Share from when you were young."

"Okay, this story's *a lot* like yours," my dad tells me. "My neighborhood when I was in middle school matched here. Mostly white with only a few who were . . ." Dad pauses.

I finish his sentence. "Black. Like us."

Dad nods a *yeah, yeah.*

Dad calls me straight Black even though I'm mixed. He's always saying, *You need to accept how the world sees you. As a Black boy.* And I do because I know what he means, even if my mom always calls me "mixed" because she's white.

Anyway, right now, Dad clears his throat. "So one of my best friends when I was your age was this Irish

kid, Pat. We'd bike so much through our neighborhood that we got 'bike butt' and walked funny."

My dad and I laugh.

"One day we go in a supermarket to get chips.
Pat opens and eats from his bag before we're at
the cashier. Like you, I figured, *Why not?* As soon
as I bite one, what happens? This lady actually yells
about me. 'He's stealing!'"

"She did that in front of the whole store, right?"

"Yes."

"How'd you feel?"

"Maybe the way you did. Low. Confused about
why only I got in trouble."

"Exactly."

Dad points at me. "To be a *boy*. Voice not even
past puberty—I could've sang in a girls' a capella
group. Bone-skinny too. But treated like I'm a grown
thug." Dad chuckles. "Crazy, huh? How you and I got
the same treatment and white kids got the opposite.
You see a pattern?"

"Yeah, and Dan wasn't scared to talk back to that
man."

"I bet. Back then, my dad had one of his longest
talks ever with me." Dad changes his voice, and it's
wild how him and my grandpa sound the same. "We
can't do everything our white friends can. You have
to think twice before you act once."

Dad's dad—my grandpa—isn't alive. When he was, my dad joked and called him Soda Pop. He told me he nicknamed Grandpa that because Grandpa kept a lot bottled in.

Right now, I ask, "Did racist stuff happen to Grandpa when he was my age?"

"*Way* more than us. He grew up in a horrible time."

"He told you about what he went through?"

Dad shakes his head. "No. And the little I do know, I *only* know from my mother. Because Dad was Soda Pop, you know? He never really had full talks with me—he just leaked what he wanted me to know, like rules with cops: 'Watch it with them,' and 'If you're in the front seat of a car and they ever pull it over, put your hands on the dashboard and keep them there. Even stick both hands out the window to let them know no weapons are in your hands. Don't give cops an excuse to . . .'"

Now I'm angrier than before.

I stare at my bracelet, at the glow-in-the-dark words WHAT LANE?

I ask Dad, "So you're saying I should stay in my lane? White boys can do stuff but I ca—?"

"That's not what I'm saying."

"Good. Because the whole world is my lane."

"Listen, Stephen, you don't want to be in prejudiced people's lanes because that puts you in their hands, and if they have you where they want you, they'll hurt you."

"That supermarket man, though? I thought store workers are supposed to be friendly to all customers."

"Not everyone who is supposed to be friendly is. And not everyone who acts friendly is your friend."

Mom pokes her head in my bedroom door. From her face, I think she's been listening for a while.

"Honey, can you come outside?" she asks Dad.

Dad stands, eyeing me. "We'll finish this later."

My door shuts and I sit back, reading the words on my bracelet again. WHAT LANE?

I swear under my breath to myself:

I'll do what I want.
I'll do everything Dan does.
I'll do everything Chad does.
I'm as good as Dan.
I'm better than Chad.
Stay in my lane? Really? What lane?

CHAPTER **8**

LATER THAT NIGHT, I need to pee. The bathroom is down the hall from my parents' bedroom.

I tiptoe by their room real quiet so I don't wake them. But they're up.

"He's too young." Mom's voice is snappy. "I don't want Stephen thinking about these things."

They're talking about me? I lean close to their door.

"Can't I just sleep?" Dad sighs hard. "Do we really need to discuss this now?"

"Yes."

"Fine." It sounds like he sits up. "You don't want him thinking about these things. But it's *happening* to him. That's why I told him what I said."

"But you're pushing him to think like an adult. He's an innocent kid."

"Me? I'm not the one bursting his bubble. The

world's doing that. You don't want him thinking like an adult? Then go tell the world to stop treating him like an adult felon. You don't want me to be like my father and bottle it all in, do you? I told myself if I had a son, I'd try to really talk with him—not just give him bits and pieces of the truth. Don't you want me to have a more open relationship with Stephen?"

"I do, but also, I want to protect him feeling free—his imagination, his mind."

It goes quiet in their room for a few seconds. Then Dad says, "I want to protect him too. I want to protect his body. From prejudiced people hurting him. He needs to know how to steer through this world as a Black boy."

"He's mixed."

"Mixed? You think a racist person sees he's mixed? And even if they did, then what? They'll give him a pass?"

He changes his voice to serious-professional. "Oh, excuse me. I didn't know you were *mixed*. You're now free to go. And remember, you can now get away with what white kids get away with. SWOOSH! There you go. Your White Skin Privilege powers have been turned on. Little boy, your force field against racism is now up."

"What's with the jokes?" Mom's voice is upset.

"I tried to be serious and explain it. You didn't get how serious it is. So maybe you'd understand it better as a joke."

"Listen . . ." My mom must be standing, because the bed creaks and her feet shuffle.

I'm ready to run fast if she comes toward the door.

My mom keeps talking. "I know that you and Stephen are Black males. I know that you go through things that I don't. I get it. Let's just go to bed and talk more tomorrow."

⇆

I lie back in bed and think about what I just heard my parents say.

I wonder why it's such a big deal for my mom to call me "mixed" when my dad's right: It's obvious I get treated foul because I'm Black.

I think back to a third-grade parent-teacher conference with my white teacher, Ms. North.

I heard Ms. North give my mom the biggest, warmest hello when my mom walked in before us. "Oh, hi! Whose parent are you?"

Then Ms. North's jaw dropped for a second when

my dad and I walked in. She acted so awkward the whole meeting and mostly spoke to my mom.

Leaving the conference, in the hall outside my class, I joked to my dad, "Ms. North looked SOS when Mom walked in."

Dad put his arm around me and rapped, all jokey. "That's because you're Black, you're Black. You're Blackity-Black-Black and you're Black. Ms. North expected your Black mom to walk in. She didn't think your mom and I'd be so . . . opposite."

Friends have said that before: *Your mom and dad are opposite.*

If you look at their skin colors, then, yeah, they're opposite. And sometimes Dad is louder and more outgoing than Mom.

But they're more similar than opposite.

My mom helps manage a public library. Dad's a teacher. And when they get into talking about books, they finish each other's sentences like they're one person. They love the same singers, shows, and restaurants. Love and hate the same politicians. You name it: They're similar.

Back then, after that parent-teacher conference, we drove home and I asked Dad, "You really think Ms. North thought you and Mom were opposites?"

My mom tried to shut it down. "Honey, this isn't

appropriate to talk badly about Stephen's teacher."

"Wait. What?" Dad said. "How am I the inappropriate one? She's the one that couldn't get over Stephen having a white mom. And a Black da—"

Mom interrupted. "Well, *now* she'll know he's mixed."

"Right, but what about his future teachers who haven't met us? Will they see Stephen as a white boy or a Black boy? And what if a cop sees Stephen? Will the cop see a white boy or a Black boy?"

She shook her head. "This again."

"Yes, *this* again. Because *this* racism thing isn't going away. So it's *appropriate* for Stephen to know some people will treat him different in this world just because he looks different. He needs to be woke so he avoids getting hurt or let down."

My mom nodded, agreeing with him. Then she giggled. "*Woke?* That doesn't even sound like you."

Dad giggled back. "Yeah. I thought the same thing as I said it."

I was thinking the same too, but "woke" is cool.

Right then, they both started smiling at each other. "Woke," they sighed, and giggled at the same time.

See? They're not opposites, really.

Now I think to fifteen minutes ago, when my mom said, *I want to protect him.* Then Dad said the same. *I want to protect him too.* They both want to protect me, so—boom—they're also the same that way.

But protect me? Do I need it?

I stare above at the solar system Dad hung from strings on the ceiling. He bought it in Manhattan's American Museum of Natural History. After he hung it up, he winked at me and said, "The world is yours."

Right now, I don't feel that way.

CHAPTER **9**

SO, THE NEXT afternoon, I can't believe it when it happens.

Me and Dan are walking and he soft-smacks my face. Boom. We start slap-boxing.

This is how we sometimes play. If one of us soft-smacks the other, it's on. We start boxing like two UFC fighters or Creed.

Right now, I bob and weave. *Swing.* "You think you better than me?"

Dan blocks like whoa. *Swing.* He misses. "Watch me beat you."

"Beat me?" I say something I heard Muhammad Ali say: "I float like a butterfly, sting like a bee!" *Swing, swing.*

He skips around me, drops his guard! *Swing. Bap.* I tag his cheek.

Kids our age walk by and a few hawk us as we slap like two cats pawing each other in those GIFs.

Then a woman's voice barks at me. "Young man! Leave that boy alone!"

Yo! *Why's she yelling at me?*

What happens next is so wild, I feel outside of myself seeing it happen.

"Go back to *your* neighborhood. Don't bring trouble here," she tells me.

Huh? She thinks I can't live here since it's a mostly white neighborhood and I'm Black. And she thinks I'm trouble.

The man with her talks to Dan. "Are you okay? Did he hurt you? Should we call the cops?"

"WHOA!" Dan interrupts them. "This is my best friend. We're *playing.*"

The look on the couple's faces—their minds won't let them believe me and Dan are tight.

The lady's head jerks back. "Oh."

The guy's slit eyes still stay on me like I'm no good.

They walk off, and Dan hangs an arm around me. "What's up *their* butts? They think they cops or something."

I shrug. "I don't know."

"And why they ask me if *I* was okay? Don't they know I'm better than you?" he jokes.

"Better?" I ask Dan. "Hold up. How you better than me?"

"What?"

"You said you better than me."

"In slap-boxing."

I feel like I'm bugging. Maybe making this about something more. But I have to ask. "Besides slap-boxing, we the same. Equal, right?"

"Yeah. Of course we're equal. Why?" Dan scans my face. "You good, Stephen?"

I lift my fist for Dan to bump. "Dead it, bruh. I'm good. We good."

He fist-bumps me. "Good. Because I might have to slap you again." He jumps, jokey, to slap-box some more.

"Nah," I tell him. "Not here."

CHAPTER 10

THE NEXT DAY, I'm at the water fountain between classes when Wes—my Black friend—comes up. We haven't hung in a while.

Dan and him have avoided each other since their beef from last year, when me and Wes were arguing about rap music.

"Drake is the best rapper out," Wes said.

I wagged my head. "He's a'ight. But he's trash compared to—"

Dan jumped in. "Wes, there's, like, twenty rappers better than Drake."

Wes snapped on Dan. "No one asked you. Rap is a *Black* thing. Let me and Stephen speak."

Ever since, they haven't spoken.

Right now, Wes is with Devin, Erik, and Elijah. These four are *tight*-tight.

What's funny is we all could pass for family,

even though we're not all half African American and white. Me, Wes, and Erik are. Devin is Dominican and Elijah is Puerto Rican.

"Whattup," I say. Me, Wes, and the other guys fist-bump. "What's good?"

"What you doing after school?" Wes asks. "We hitting the bowling alley. Come."

"Dang, I have plans," I say because I'm broke, plus I don't feel like bowling.

"Word?" Wes rolls his eyes. "You mean you and Dan have plans, right?"

I'm glad Dan isn't here. Because Dan would ask Wes, "Why you roll your eyes when you say my name?"

Wes thumbs his nose. "Let me talk with you, on the low."

I'm confused. "A'ight."

He asks Devin, Erik, and Elijah, "Wait here?"

⇆

When we're far enough from Devin, Erik, and Elijah, Wes asks me in a soft voice, "Bruh, why you only be with white kids now?"

"*Whoa.* What?"

"You. You always with Dan, and Jen, Christopher, and Jeremiah."

"If I only hang with them, how am I here with you?"

"This ain't hanging." He names times he's seen me with Dan, Jen, and all them lately. "*That* is hanging. And they all white."

I chuckle. "So? They white. And me and you just hung last . . ." Oh snap. I can't even remember when. "Hold up. We last hung out . . ."

He raises an eyebrow. "Go 'head."

"Wait. Me, you, and Devin hit the arcade. That was just . . ."

He finishes my sentence, all flat. "A month ago. Look at you. You can't even really name when we last hung."

"Yeah." I feel grimy because I like Wes. "We should link up. Mos' def."

"We *should*. So don't run from us." He pauses. "Because we alike, y'feel me?"

"Alike?"

"Black. Brown."

Here we go again. "Black." Like my dad says, I'm only "Black." This feels like my dad saying I need to stay in my lane.

"So I should stay in one lane?" I ask. "The Black lane?"

"Nah, bruh. I'm saying ride in mad lanes. But you only in one now. With some grimy heads."

"*Grimy?* Grimy why? Who's grimy? Dan? He's not grimy just because you don't like him."

"You think I don't like Dan. Dan's okay, just nosy. Chad's the one who's grimy."

I didn't know they had history. "Why Chad? What'd he do?"

Wes take a deep breath and explains. "So, when Chad first started here, I was friendly to him. One day, we walked out near each other at dismissal, and his parents were outside waiting for him. I said bye and he ignored me. I stuck around to talk with a friend who wasn't too far from Chad, and I overheard his parents say . . ."

"What?"

"His pops asked him, real disgusting, 'Who is *that?*' And Chad said, *just* as disgusting, 'A nobody. That's Dan's friend.' His pops told him, 'Make sure. I don't want to see you with kids like that.' And his mom *nodded*, agreeing with his pops!"

I ask, "What they mean by 'kids like that'?"

"That's what I'm saying! Was I cursing? Was I being a troublemaker? No! His dad could've only meant one thing by 'kids like that'—Black kids."

"Wow, Wes, they were foul."

"It gets worse. Then about a week later, a few of us were at the park playing Hands. Me, Elijah, and some white kids Elijah knew. So Chad and his friends—Andy and Gabe—came over. Chad asked to play, so me and him started, right?

"He puts his open hands on mine and I'm on the bottom. *Smack.* I smack his. *Smack smack.* I keep soft-smacking the back of his hands over and over, real easy. He gets lucky and pulls away once. Since I missed, it's his turn to try and smack my hands. On his turn, he OD's. He smacks my hands way too hard. His friends Andy and Gabe grin all evil. Then he keeps hitting me, harder and harder. I tell him, 'Chad, chill,' but homeboy keeps trying to smack my hands *off*."

Wes's face right now. Tight doesn't even describe it. He eyes me like I'm Chad and he wants to snuff me.

"That's so messed up. What you do?" I say.

"I pulled my hands back and asked, 'Why you keep OD smacking hard when I said chill?!' Chad's friend Andy asked me, 'What if Chad punched you in the face. What would you do?' And I told him, 'I'd knock his teeth out. And if you jumped in, I'd knock *your* teeth out.'"

Wes isn't a troublemaker. But he's not afraid to fight if he has to, even if the person is bigger. It happened when this eighth grader named Keith and his friend tried bullying Wes by soft-smacking his neck without knowing him. I wasn't there, but I heard Wes dropped Keith with one punch. Everyone knows about it.

"So that's when Chad and them left. To avoid getting their butts beat."

"Woooow. I didn't know."

Talk about weird timing. Right now, Chad turns a corner, spots me talking to Wes, and then U-turns around the corner he came from.

"Son," Wes says. "See? He's butt. That's why he just U-turned. *Never* bring him near me. And you should watch out with him. Dude'll go too far if you let him."

I nod, staring Wes in the eye. It feels like he has my back.

I lift my fist. "Let's get up with each other soon. For real. All of us: you, Devin, Erik, Elijah."

He nods. "Word."

As our fists bump, I notice he rocks a black rubber bracelet like mine. I nod at the white letters on his. "What's BLM?"

"Bruh, *for real?*" He shakes his head like he can't believe I asked that. "*Black Lives Matter.* The fact you don't know means you *should* hang with us more."

It's like he's saying again that I'm riding too much in one lane—a white lane. It's like he's saying I'm slipping on being Black.

⇆

I don't like looking ignorant, so later in computer lab, I type in *Black lives matter*. Dang! This page is full of links. Now I feel extra dumb for being clueless about it. I won't be next time. I read parts of different links in my head.

Social movement . . . that the lives of Blacks matter . . .

A group saying life should be just as fair for Blacks as everyone else . . .

Black Lives Matter . . . mantra for people protesting police violence against Blacks . . .

Life should be just as fair for Blacks as everyone else.

This is so similar to what I've been thinking about. Life should be the same for me as it is for my white friends.

So me and Wes's bracelets sorta mean the same thing?

CHAPTER 11

WHEN DAN AND I get to the park on Sunday, everyone's there, including Chad. *Why isn't he with his friends?* I wonder. *Why's he with us on the regular now?*

Chad sees me and his face says the same thing I feel about him: *Why're you even here?*

Then, from high up, Christopher calls and jokes to me, "Stephen Curry!"

I smile because it's wavy being called that, and Christopher's a'ight. Plus it's dope he's climbed to the top of the fence that cages in the handball court. He dangles a leg over like it's dumb easy to be up there.

Chad dares me, "Bet you can't climb it too."

I eye the fence's holes, so small that sneakers' fronts barely fit in them. *How'd Christopher climb this?*

I'm about to ask Christopher when Chad hisses, "Don't ask Christopher. He climbed it on his own when I dared *him*. You don't need help either."

Fine. I go for it and my fingers carry most of my weight, since my feet won't grip. My fingers *hurt-hurt*, and halfway up, the pain makes me want to come down.

I look at Christopher waving me up. I look down at Chad smile-yelling, "If you can't climb it, just come down!"

I can do what any of these guys can do, I think. I keep climbing.

Now my friends cheer me on.

Jeremiah: "Stephen, you got this!"

Jen: "You're almost there!"

Dan: "C'mon, Miles Morales! Reach the top!"

I glance back down. When you're two stories up with nothing to catch you, two stories feels like way more.

But now I'm amped to get to the top.

And Chad hates that. He jumps on the fence and starts shaking it.

Here's the thing: My fingers have that feeling of carrying heavy plastic shopping bags by the handles for too long multiplied by a million. Now Chad's climbing this fence, shaking it, and I'm losing my grip.

"Stop, Chad!" Jen yells. "You're gonna make Stephen fall!"

Christopher reaches out to me from the top. "Stephen, give me your hand. I'll pull you up."

I grip my fingers into fence holes and pull myself up as hard as I can.

Christopher's hand is now *so* close. "Stephen, a little more. Just a little."

Right then—*smack*—our hands clasp, and with me climbing and him pulling, I make it to the top.

All of a sudden, Chad loses interest and jumps down.

Me and Christopher dangle one foot over. "Dan called you Miles. Spider-Man Miles?"

"Yeah."

"Then you're Miles, for real. This climb isn't easy."

"Don't try gassing Stephen's head up!" Chad jealous-shouts at us celebrating. "He's no real climber."

Dan's annoyed voice checks Chad. "You're talking? You didn't even make it to the top."

"'Cause I didn't want to," Chad replies. "It's too easy a climb. And, Stephen, if you're Miles, let's all go to the factory. Show us how to climb that fence."

I don't want to go there, but Chad's smirk annoys me. And it's gonna feel good wiping the smirk off his face when I punk him by getting through the fence without even climbing it.

When I say, "Yeah. I'll go," Chad smiles big at me—the kind the Joker gives Batman.

CHAPTER **12**

WHEN I SEE the NO TRESPASSING signs around the factory, my dad's advice from Grandpa Soda Pop plays in my head. *Think twice before you act once.*

Yeah, they'd both tell me that now about going in here.

Whatevs, I think. *I can handle this.*

The sky gets darker as I study the fence. *Is the opening I saw last time at this bottom here? Or that bottom?*

Jeremiah tells Jen, "Kinda creepy how this place is next to a cemetery, huh?"

I crouch and yank the fence, but it won't lift. I rush to another spot, yank, it lifts, and I yell to my friends, "Why climb when we can roll under?"

Everyone is SOS because they never thought of that.

I hold up the fence and Dan wiggles under fast. One by one, everyone does.

Now I'm the last one outside.

A faraway cop siren whistles, making me pause a second. I remember, *Everyone is white here but me.*

"You coming?" Dan asks. "I can't hold this fence up forever."

I wiggle under.

⇆

I was right about getting inside the factory too—the lock on the door is all for show. When we pull the door back hard, there's enough room for each of us to slip through by turning sideways.

I expected inside the factory to be scary, and it is. Long shadows stretch off tall metal machines—the shadows remind me of those monsters from the *Shazam!* movie that stood still, waiting to come alive. Wind howls through busted windows, making newspaper pages and plastic bags swirl, alive-like, around our feet.

We're not the first ones in here. Old mattresses are on the ground in two different spots with empty bottles near them. Graffiti is on walls. Doesn't help relax me that some are demons and skulls.

But it's the clanking sound that really freaks me out—like someone is banging a warning. No one has to tell me I have frightened googly eyes. I feel them.

Dan feels like I do. He comes and whispers in my ear, "That noise. You think it's ghosts telling us to get out?"

Then Chad points to two conveyor belts that slope up in a forty-five-degree angle to some square holes near the ceiling.

"How sick would it be to climb way up there? I bet we fit through those holes. Let's climb them," Chad dares us.

"Nah. We could fall. Look how high those belts slope," Jeremiah says.

Chad eyes me the way he did back at the handball court fence. "Stephen, you think you're Spider-Man. You said you're a climber. Race me."

Christopher cuts him off. "I'll race you, Chad. And you know I'll dust you."

Chad gets competitive. "C'mon, then."

They go.

I'm glad Christopher just saved me—but I don't want him getting hurt. Still, if anyone's got this, it's him. His climbing skills are tight.

Chad scoots onto one conveyor belt, Christopher on the other.

"On your mark," they both say at the same time, "get set, GO!"

They race up, and the higher they get, the bouncier the conveyor belts get.

Jeremiah yells up to them, "Slow down!" He turns to us. "Dang! They're about to bounce off!"

I'm scared just watching, and only when Christopher makes it to the top and through a ceiling square do I relax. Chad follows and then is gone too.

Jen says, "C'mon. If they can do it, we can." She climbs on a belt and starts up. Her climbing skills are awesome too. Her brother, Jeremiah, scrambles to keep up with her.

Me and Dan turn to each other.

"I guess I'm doing it." Dan climbs on.

Ugh! Now I *have* to.

I climb behind him, and he tells me, "Quit bouncing."

"That's *you*."

These belts are *not* stable. The higher we get, the bouncier they get, and the more I need to focus on not falling off.

Jeremiah and Jen wait for us and we all keep going forward.

We're almost at the square openings where Chad and Christopher disappeared, when—

"BOO!" Chad pops his head out and snaps a photo. The flash is blinding.

I stumble but catch myself as Jen screams at him, "You IDIOT!"

But Jeremiah . . .

When he jumped back from Chad's flash, one of his legs slipped off the conveyor belt. Now they're both dangling off the belt.

Everyone's eyes pop and stare at him.

I imagine the worst. Him letting go and breaking both legs when he hits the floor.

Jen scoots back to help her brother, but—good thing—he's okay. He swings a leg up that catches the conveyor belt. Then his other. His whole body shifts back on.

Phew.

We all climb through the square openings, and Jen's so mad, she yells, "What's wrong with you, Chad?!"

Dan's mad too. "Chad, you could've killed one of us! Not! Cool!"

"Shut up." Chad swats away them criticizing him. "No one got hurt."

He walks off into the shadows.

CHAPTER **13**

IT'S DARKER UP on this next floor.

Jen's cooled down from being so mad. She asks her brother, "Take a picture of me in front of the window. The glass shards behind me look creepy, right?"

Goose bumps rise on my body. Maybe it's the howling wind? Maybe the nonstop metal clanking? Maybe both?

It's like Dan reads my mind. "Stephen, each clank sounds like, *GO HOME! Go home.*"

"I know," I say. "If you said someone is behind that door over there slamming a pipe against something, I'd believe you."

Dan squints at the closed rusty door across the room. He whispers so just I can hear. "Want to leave?"

I eye my bracelet. The words glow in the dark: **WHAT LANE?** Yeah, maybe *not* this lane now. I nod at Dan. "Yeah. Let's leave."

All of a sudden, the clanking gets louder and faster. Jeremiah, Jen, and Christopher stare at the door with the same shook eyes as us.

Dan tells them, "Anyone else ready to bounce? Me and Stephen are out."

They nod, and we head to an old metal staircase.

Chad spots us and starts dissing. "This place too much for y'all? You should see yourselves. Ready to run."

Jen grabs her brother's arm. "Chad, forget you."

"C'mon, Chad," Dan says. "Just come with us. We've seen enough of here."

But Chad doesn't move, so we leave him behind.

We go slowly, feeling which steps are safe. We didn't come up this way, so we see new stuff as we head down the staircase.

Dan spots what looks like a fireman's pole. "Hey, maybe it'd be faster sliding down that."

Jeremiah squints at it. "Yeah. Next time. Nah. Forget here. No next time."

We finally reach the bottom and pass a huge pool full of Styrofoam balls.

"Whoa," Christopher says. "Wanna jump in? That'd be crazy."

"Yeah, but not good crazy," Jeremiah says. "I'm not trying to get ringworm or lice. Our mom would love us bringing home weird bugs."

But Christopher's already walking toward the Styrofoam pool. So is Jen.

Then she screams.

Christopher smacks his hand to his mouth. "YOoooo, an arm is in there!"

We all inch toward the pool. A lifeless arm floats in the pool of Styrofoam.

We all stand there, scared.

Dan: "Do you think a body's attached?"

Jeremiah: "If we find a dead body, the police have to get involved."

Jen: "Our parents too."

Christopher: "What if the cops think we killed this person?"

I'm shook and my mind races. What'll happen if a cop comes? *Everyone here is white and I'm not.* I remember how Junior—my super—swore I knew that bike thief. He saw Dan as innocent and me as guilty because I'm Black.

I was afraid a minute ago, and now a whole other fear hits me. I want to run.

CHAPTER 14

ME AND DAN'S eyes meet, and we swallow so hard, our Adam's apples pump.

It seems time froze in this factory. The clanging hasn't stopped. Now there's a body.

Everyone looks scared and confused as we discuss what to do.

Then all of a sudden . . .

"AAAAH!" The dead arm comes to life and flings Styrofoam at us.

We jump back, run . . . and then realize . . .

It's Chad.

"Come in for a swim, scaredy-cats," he jokes.

"YOoooo, I almost peed on myself," Jeremiah says.

Jen shakes her head. "Again with the rude surprises, Chad?"

Christopher is confused. "How'd you get down here before us?"

Chad points at the fireman's pole. "Slid down that."

Christopher says, "Too bad you didn't fall off it and get sense knocked into you."

He turns and heads for the door leading out of the factory. One by one we follow him. Even Chad climbs out and runs to catch up to us while laughing and making fun of our reactions.

I hang back so I don't have to hear him. Jeremiah starts walking with me.

"'Sup?" I ask Jeremiah.

"Nothing. It's just . . . Chad being Chad, I guess."

"Yeah, he's too extra," I tell Jeremiah. "But I was worried you'd fall off that belt and get hurt. Like, *seriously* hurt."

I see just enough of the side of Jeremiah's face to know he's glad I care.

He whispers back, "Me too. I didn't even want to climb it."

"So why did you?" I ask.

"Once Chad started it, everyone rode that lane. How'd I look if I punked out?"

"I get it," I tell him. "I was right there riding in Chad's lane too."

CHAPTER **15**

THE NEXT DAY in school, when any of them see me, they call me over.

Each time it's the same: "Yo, how scary was . . . ?" or "Remember when we . . . ?" or "It was kray when . . ."

"Yeah." I shrug, nod, or smile, then leave fast.

Just knowing I went in that factory feels enough. And today I replayed it in my head and thought, *You wouldn't've been in the same lane as them if cops caught you in the factory.* I tried to kill that idea: *You're bugging—cops would've been fair.*

But what my grandpa Soda Pop told my dad about cops . . .

Would cops have been fair?

Those thoughts bug me and I wished they'd stop.

So when Dan calls out to me before we go in the lunchroom, the last thing I want is for him to go ape about the factory.

And he doesn't.

Not for *all* of lunch.

It's wild how he's the opposite of everyone about the factory, so as we leave the lunchroom for upstairs, I say, "Heads can't quit bragging about that factory, huh?"

"For real." He stops, looks to make sure no one hears, and leans in. "They're too extra. We broke in, right? That should be enough. It was even sorta dumb that we did. And *Chad* . . ."

I wait.

"Chad's . . . sometimes . . ."

I keep waiting.

"How'd you describe him again?"

"Wack."

"Yeah, that and more."

"Opposite of you?"

"Yeah, it's hard to believe we're cousins sometimes."

"You can't say that," I tell him.

"Why not?"

"Because I'm the one who said it first and told you. You copying me."

He soft-punches my arm. "Ha, ha. But you were right."

I feel better knowing Dan gets it about Chad.

I want to tell him, *You know. So what now?* But the nine-year-old shy me pulls me back. We'll see.

CHAPTER **16**

EVER SINCE WES told me about Black Lives Matter, I've heard and seen stuff about it here and there.

Our school has this new Reading Partners program with a high school across the street, and our English teacher, Mr. Diaz, signed my class up for it. So a little after lunch, we walk over. What's the first thing I see in the hall? A Black Lives Matter bulletin board.

Tons of photos on half the board. I try moving around kids in my class to see better. *Dang, why they just standing, blocking me? They're not even looking at the board.*

I finally get to it. One photo has a white teenage guy holding a poster with the question IS MY LIFE WORTH MORE THAN HIS? An arrow on his poster points to a Black guy his age holding a poster too. His question is IS MY LIFE WORTH LESS THAN HIS?

His arrow points at the white guy. There's another photo of a Black woman holding a poster with the question IS MY SON NEXT? I think about the things my dad said about racist people and about Grandpa Soda Pop having it real-*real* rough.

My eyes go to another part of the board. A photo shows a boy who looks like Wes. Underneath his photo are typed words:

TAMIR RICE
Age: 12. R.I.P. 2014.
Unarmed & shot dead by police.
Tamir could be your little brother.
How do you feel about what happened
in Cleveland, Ohio?

I squint at different-colored Post-its in handwriting like mine with high school students' answers to that question. WOOOOW! A white cop shot this kid. And the kids here are *pissed* about it!

Another photo grabs my eye: Colin Kaepernick in his football uniform on one knee during the National Anthem. Underneath, the big typed questions ask,

What does Colin Kaepernick taking a knee say about there being two different Americas?

What does his taking a knee have to do with Black Lives Matter?

I stare at all the Post-its with handwritten answers to those questions. I lean in to read one when Mr. Diaz calls my name from across the hall and shocks me. I jump.

Oh dip! Like, almost my whole class has turned and disappeared around the corner. I run to catch up, and while I run, I wish my class was headed into that classroom with the Black Lives Matter bulletin board outside. This makes me think two things. First, it'd be cool to hear what high school students think about BLM. Second, it reminds me of Wes and how I told him we should hang. And we should.

After school, I whip out my cell and hit him up.

CHAPTER **17**

EARLIER, WHEN I told my dad that I called Wes and he invited me over for dinner, my dad glad-clapped. "Date night for your mom and me!"

Right now, my parents watch me leave our car and walk to Wes, who waits outside his building for me and waves at them. They'll get me later.

We both live in Brooklyn, but Wes's neighborhood is more mixed than ours.

"Stephen, where have you been?" Wes's mom is at their apartment door and hugs me like I'm family.

"Stephen!" Wes's dad stands from the sofa, his voice happy. "When Wes said you'd visit, I didn't believe it, stranger! Figured you and your Golden State Warriors were flying state to state to win us the championship." Mr. Campbell—Wes's dad—is a Stephen Curry fan for real. He rubs his wrists to massage the pain out and waves at the table in front of his sofa. "Tired of figuring out these Halloween decorations and how to cut this pumpkin. You boys take over. Small pumpkins here to draw on too."

Wes's dad leaves for another room. Me and Wes go sit on the sofa.

"So?" Wes asks. "Want to?"

I nod. "Sure," I tell him. "Halloween is what's up."

On the table are a bunch of fist-size pumpkins, Sharpies in every color, and a huge pumpkin Wes's dad didn't even start cutting.

I point at the Sharpies. "Want to draw faces on the small pumpkins?"

Wes's face lights up. He has an idea. "Has to be pumpkin-drawing videos we can watch." He checks on his phone and taps one.

The vlogger's hair reminds me of Shawn Mendes. "Okay, let's draw a pumpkin face to really freak people out," the dude says. "Got your Sharpies?"

Me and Wes eye each other. "Word."

We watch teen Sharpie Shawn Mendes draw circles. I can draw those. Then he says, "Then, with your Sharpie, add this shading . . ."

Me and Wes cock our heads sideways, trying to figure out what the dude is drawing.

Sharpie dude keeps on. "Then swish these bags under the eyes . . . real easy to do, y'know?"

No, I don't know. He makes it look easy—it's not.

He keeps drawing and then holds up his finished pumpkin. "Boom. How fly is this?"

My jaw drops. "He's gotta do animation for Marvel or something."

Wes's face is just as Stuck On Stupid as mine. "Or Disney. Who draws on his level?" He picks up his phone again. "Let's find something easier. No disrespect."

"Nah. I don't feel dissed. Go 'head."

Wes scrolls three under and taps on the link. "Boom."

This teenage girl might be mixed—Asian and something—and sounds like Peni Parker from *Into the Spider-Verse*. "Okayee. You'll need glitter for theeeese pumpkins . . ."

Glitter?

Me and Wes say at the same time, "Skip."

Wes scrolls down. A video title says, *Drawing pumpkins for kindergarten.*

Me and Wes slow-shrug at each other, half-jokey, half-serious.

"I mean," I say, "I'm down if you're down."

Wes sigh-laughs. "Whew! Glad you said that."

He presses Play, and this video is *just* our speed. We grab pumpkins and Sharpies, aim our marker tips, and follow the video step-by-step.

A face starts forming on mine. I check—on Wes's too.

We keep drawing. I want to say, *Wes, bruh. Us hanging again is cool.* Shy me holds back. Then I decide to go for it. "Wes, us chilling again is . . ."

His nod and little smile back tell me I don't have to say anything else. He feels how I do. He finishes my sentence. "Is cool, right?"

"Yeah."

He lifts his pumpkin, which looks like someone younger than kindergarten scribbled all over it. He chuckles. "Us hanging is better than my pumpkin."

I hold up my cross-eyed, jacked-up pumpkin too. "*And* mine."

We laugh and can't stop for a while; then we lift up our hands for a fist bump.

When we do, our bracelets touch and stay connected for a few seconds. BLM. WHAT LANE? Seeing these phrases together feels right.

CHAPTER 18

"THAT HOUSE IS all-the-way Halloweened out!" I tell Dan as I point at this brownstone building. It's the day after me and Wes hung out. "That house wins."

We're walking and ranking buildings with the dopest Halloween decorations.

"Give me reasons why," he says.

"Boom. To start, see that scary-scary witch in the window?"

"Yeah."

"Check out her hands and face. Her lizardy fingers with the long, sharp nails curling back like hawk claws grabbing prey? And the light shining on her half-rotted green face? Sonnnn!"

"Yo!" Dan cups his fist to his mouth. "She *is* scary!"

"Bam," I say. "But peep her bulging eyes staring at what she's about to grab."

Dan squints. "Is that a kid in front of her?"

"Yup. And terrified, right?"

"That's *wiiiild*. He's about to become dinner!"

I put on a scary witch voice: *"C'mere, little boy. You tasty-looking!"*

"This whole house is OD scary."

We keep on, taking turns pointing out more.

Dan: "The whole thing is in cobwebs."

Me: "Cut-off heads hanging from different windows."

Dan: "Human-size zombies in her gate."

Me: "The signs saying, 'This way to the afterlife.'"

"Yep. That house is the scariest." Dan sighs. "I wish Halloween was every day. I like that the whole world acts like us on Halloween. They get into fantasy stuff and act like your bracelet."

I look down at my WHAT LANE? bracelet. "What you mean?"

"The whole year, everyone acts one way. In one lane. But for Halloween, everyone is in different lanes, being whoever or whatever they want to be."

"Facts."

We pass the comic store, and spooky Halloween masks stare at us through the window.

"Hold up," I tell Dan.

Some comic stores be like, *Look, don't touch.* Not this place. It's lit. The owner doesn't care if we stay for hours reading *too* many comics to name. He even lets us play with stuff. Once, me and Dan tried on *Star Wars* robes and dueled in the comic aisles with lightsabers, making sound effects.

Only thing the owner says every now and then is "You break it, you bought it."

We go in and Dan tries on a werewolf mask. "Grrrr . . ."

I point. "The front of the mask's face is all crushed in. Our faces almost ended up looking that way."

He pulls it off. "When?"

"In the factory. When Chad snapped photos of us at the top of the conveyor belt." I point at the mask's crushed-in face. "That would've been us."

Dan twists his lips to the side and gets kind of quiet. "Yeah."

I say, "We could've gotten hurt-hurt."

He hangs the mask back on its hook. "For real." The way he soft-says it, I know he agrees, even though he wishes he didn't.

I've been wondering things.

This is a moment: I feel it—I can do my New Year's resolution or be the little nine-year-old me and not speak up. I look at him, wondering if I should. Whatevs.

"Dan, you ever go with the crowd and do something and think it's fun, then after you think back, you feel differently?"

"Yeah. You know I felt that about when we raced up those conveyor belts."

"Can I speak my mind? Keep it a hundred?"

He nods.

"Did it look like I was having fun when I climbed that fence after Christopher did?"

"Yeah, like Miles when he flipped off that building, all free and happy."

"I was, but wasn't. I was trying to prove I wasn't in one lane. That I could be in Christopher's. But really, I did it for Chad."

His face wrinkles, confused. "Chad? He didn't even climb that fence."

"Yeah, but he was the one to dare me. And then on the conveyor belt too. I talked to Jeremiah a little about it that day. We felt grimy because we were really just in Chad's lane. So we weren't free at all."

Dan nods slowly, over and over. "Chad's lane . . ." He points at the werewolf mask's crushed-in face and chuckles a not-funny laugh. "End up messed up in Chad's lane."

CHAPTER **19**

I'M ON DAN'S swively chair watching *Stranger Things* the next afternoon when Dan comes back and hands me a huge bowl of chips. "Chad and his parents just got here."

"Word?"

We didn't plan for Chad to come chill, but I guess that's what's gonna keep happening if your cousin moves nearby. My mind rewinds to what Wes said about Chad's parents. I haven't met them yet, and my belly sort of flips from nervousness. I don't even want to deal with Chad—now there are two super-size Chads here!

I'm curious how they look. "Hold up, Dan. Pause it."

I get up and peek through Dan's door into the living room. Wes described Chad's parents as racist, and that made me imagine them as Draco Malfoy's parents in the Harry Potter movies. I pictured them pale-pale white with bleached hair. Vampire-looking. But they're just normal. I'm shocked they look so regular.

I watch Chad and his family. Chad's saying something, but his mom's swiping on her cell and doesn't even lift her eyes to him. Chad's dad looks bored and doesn't connect with him either. It's like Chad doesn't exist to them.

For a minute I feel bad for Chad. How messed up is his family? Ignoring him. On top of his parents maybe being racist, they're icy.

I want to ask Dan about them, but I can't, because all of a sudden Chad turns to walk to Dan's room. Oh dang!

I jet to the bed. "Press Play. *Press Play!*"

"What?" Dan's confused.

"*Press. Play.* Chad's coming."

"Look at you eavesdropping and now you don't want to get caught." Dan laughs as he presses Play.

⇆

It's thirty minutes later, Chad's parents are gone, and me and Dan are into-into *Stranger Things* on the screen. Chad isn't.

I glance at Chad and he's not even watching the show. I want to be nice since I feel bad his parents were so cold—and I wouldn't want to sit through a show I'm not feeling. I decide to speak up.

"Dan, pause this."

He does.

I keep on. "Chad, you not into this show?"

He looks at me, confused. "What?"

"This is me and Dan's show, but we could watch something else if you want. Something we all like."

Usually, when someone's friendly to you, you react friendly. But Chad stares at me stone-cold. There's straight saltiness in his voice. "Why are you all in my face? Just watch your show."

Dan gets motionless-quiet and slits his eyes at Chad. His stare says, *Chad, I don't get you. Nasty now for what?*

Chad points at me, then at the screen, and throws me more shade. "What're you, scared? This scene too scary and you're using me as an excuse to pause it?"

Really? After I'm nice to him? He's grimy? I'm glad Dan sees how nasty—for no reason—Chad is to me.

I feel my neck get hotter. I remember my dad's advice: *Fires don't put out fires. Be chill to cool things off.*

I stand. "I'm going to the bathroom."

"Okay." Dan talks to his cousin. "Chad, maybe you should go too. Home. You're killing our vibe."

I smile. That's what I want. If Chad hasn't bounced by the time I'm back, I will.

CHAPTER 20

THE NEXT DAY, right after school, Chad sits on someone's car and looks like he's telling a story to Jen, Christopher, and Jeremiah.

On the sidewalk, kids go in different directions. Me and Dan stop to listen.

". . . So I told him, 'How are you dissing me when your head is shaped like a football?'" Chad says. "And the school security guard," he continues, "yesterday during the fire drill, he tripped and landed on the floor! How is he protecting us when he can't walk?"

Chad keeps cracking dis jokes. Being his usual nasty-for-no-reason. *At least he's not picking on me,* I think. But he'll probably start again.

And sure enough—boom—Chad's eyes zoom in on me. "Hey, Stephen, you're into ghosts and monsters, right? You should come see the haunted house me, Andy, and Gabe are making in Andy's basement.

We found old Halloween decorations and props no one uses. Even a used fog machine is down there."

"For real?" Jen asks. "What about witches?"

"Got that, and skeletons too. Come see it? Maybe help decorate."

Jen looks at her brother, and they answer at the same time, "Sure."

"Yeah," Christopher chimes in. "Why not?"

Chad studies my face, waiting for my answer, like he did the other day.

Halloween is about a week away. I want to be less around Chad, but his haunted house sounds cool, and if my friends are in, I'm in.

Chad taps me. "So you're in?"

"Yeah, Chad. When can you take us to Andy's?"

"Tomorrow," Chad says.

"Can't," Jen says. "My parents are taking us away after school for the weekend."

"So when?" Chad asks us.

"Next week sometime?" Christopher asks.

Dan finally speaks. "Sounds good. But, Chad, you want help fixing it? I'll come tomorrow."

"Nah, no need," Chad says. "I only threw in the idea of decorating it more because I thought you'd like that. But it's a hundred percent haunted already. Let's do this: next Friday. It's the day before Halloween, so it'll feel extra haunted Halloweeny."

We're all down. Done. Decided.

Everyone splits up to where it's just me and Dan. No Chad for once. Word.

We get to my building, and Leo, our doorman, shouts out to me, "Stephen Curry! How is your three-point shot?"

Our doorman is the opposite of our super. Leo's eyes smile when he sees me; Junior's eyes slit when he sees me. One does his best to talk to me in English even though he speaks Russian or something; the other curses at me in Spanish.

It's always funny when Leo asks me about my three-point shot, especially since I'm trash in basketball.

I smile. "Perfect!"

He points to himself and asks, "Stephen, where am I from?" Ever since he first started working here, this is a thing we do. He quizzes me to see if I remember what he told me when we met.

I say, "Kosovo."

"Where is that?"

I answer, "Europe."

As we speak, Dan pokes his hand in the plastic jack-o'-lantern Leo has on his counter for candy.

"Your Halloween decorations are nice," I tell Leo while waving at the tables, walls, and mirrors. Smiling paper pumpkins are taped on walls. A sign with cobwebs saying HAPPY HALLOWEEN is draped on the wall-to-wall mirror. Leo does a good job of making our lobby Halloweeny but *not* OD scary for the little-*little* kids who live here.

"You like my skeleton?" He points at the wall behind me.

I turn around. I'd missed it. The legs are in the air in a split pose, with one hand holding a pumpkin up like the Statue of Liberty holds her torch.

I ask, "Michael Jordan?"

"You got it! I wondered if anyone would know his pose!"

"Come on, Leo. Everyone knows that's Michael Jordan's move."

He smiles, proud of himself, and points to the plastic jack-o'-lantern of candy Dan just put down. "Take."

I peek in. Ugh. No gummy bears left. "No, thanks."

More people come into our lobby and Leo chats with them.

"Why didn't you take candy?" Dan asks me.

I shrug. "Wanted gummies. None were left."

Dan holds out a mini pack of gummy bears. "This was Leo's last."

I look in Dan's hand. "You took other candies?"

"Nah. Just these. But you can have them."

I feel it again. Dan has my back.

CHAPTER 21

WHEN I WALK in my apartment, my mom's on her laptop at the dinner table and my dad's on his on the couch. He's watching a video and taking notes, probably working on a lesson plan.

He winces at what he's watching. "I'll never get used to this crap!"

I go toward him. "What crap?"

My mom tells him, "Turn it off, please. Stephen's too young for this."

I stare at Dad's screen. A cop aims a gun at a boy my size and the boy falls.

"Stephen *should* see this," my dad tells my mom. "He's the same age as Tamir Rice. And I need to polish my lesson for tomorrow."

Tamir Rice? I read about him on that Black Lives Matter bulletin board! Now I'm more curious. I sit next to Dad.

"And the cop," my dad keeps telling her, "didn't

think Tamir was too young to be shot dead. The courts didn't think Tamir was too young to get justice. They said those cops were innocent. If Stephen is young enough to get shot by a bigot cop, he's young enough to know it's happening."

Mom stands and starts talking about me like I'm not here, and like I don't want to see this video when I do. "Honey, remember about protecting Stephen's innocence a bit longer? He's still just into fantasy and stuff."

"Do you know who else was probably just into fantasy and stuff?" he asks her. "Tamir Rice. He was a boy. Playing. With a toy gun. In a park." Dad turns and puts me on the spot. "Are you too young to know about this?"

I don't want to make my mom mad, but I want to see this video. I tell her in a real soft voice, "I already know about Tamir Rice. White cops killed him in Ohio. Can I just watch a little?"

She lifts her open hands like she says, *I give up*. She goes to their bedroom.

Dad squints at the screen. So do I.

"How do you know about Tamir?" he asks.

"My class does this Reading Partners program with a high school, and they have a Black Lives Matter bulletin board. I read some about him there."

Dad nods. "Remember a few weeks back, when I said we can't do what white folks can?"

"Yeah." I look at my bracelet.

"Tamir had a toy gun—maybe it looked real. The white cop shot him without checking to see if it was a toy."

My eyes go back to the screen. The headshot of Tamir—he looked kinda like Wes. I feel bad-bad for Tamir. And I feel mad. At the cops who killed him. Mad for other reasons I can't put into words.

"This stuff," Dad says, "it just keeps happening. Your grandpa Soda Pop had to live with it. Now you have to live with it."

I look at his face and he's . . .

. . . ZERO words can describe his face.

He's never looked how he does now. Like he could rip apart his laptop with his bare hands.

I scoot next to him, slide my arm around his back, hug him soft, and rest my head on his shoulder.

He reaches for my hand and holds it like he never wants to let me go.

⇆

At night, I lie on my bed thinking about that Tamir Rice video. We saw the whole thing. After he was shot, his older sister came to the park and tried to help him. Instead of letting her, the cops put her in handcuffs.

Jen and Jeremiah pop up in my mind. What if it was them? It'd crush Jen if Jeremiah was shot by cops. It'd kill her if cops cuffed her, keeping her from Jeremiah as he died.

Then I think again. *That wouldn't happen to them. They're in a different lane.*

CHAPTER **22**

THE NEXT DAY, I can't get Tamir Rice off my mind.

In all my morning classes, I think of him. *What was going through his head?*

In all my afternoon classes, I keep thinking of Tamir. *What's his sister going through? Did the cop who killed him get punished? If a Black cop did that, would he get the same punishment as the white cop? Why didn't that cop stop to really see Tamir?*

I check: Ms. Simmons teaches like her lesson will really help me. I pretend to listen.

I spend a lot of the time sketching block letters in the margins of my loose-leaf and shading in his name: TAMIR RICE.

Finally it's eighth-period advisory with Mr. Carrión.

We sit in the circle of chairs and he asks, "So, anything anyone wants to bring up related to what's going on in our world?"

I'm too ready. I blurt out, "Let's discuss cops shooting young unarmed Black kids."

Everyone eyes me like, *Wow! Where did THAT come from?* Especially Wes.

"A Black Lives Matter bulletin board about it is in the high school," I say.

A white girl named Elizabeth asks, all snooty, "When did cops *ever* shoot Black kids our age? Never."

Woooow. She is straight ignorant but talks all confident like an expert.

I look at Mr. Carrión, hoping he'll explain, and he does. "So you'd think cops don't shoot and kill innocent Black kids, and I wish they didn't, but the fact is, cops do."

Elizabeth's friend Brittany backs her up. "Then the kids had to do *something*. No one gets shot for no reason."

I hear my dad in my head getting upset about Tamir Rice. Words come out. "Tamir Rice was twelve. He was in a park, sitting on a picnic table like we always do. He was playing with a toy gun like a *Star Wars* soldier or something, and the gun might've looked real."

"And he was Black," Mr. Carrión adds.

"Are you saying that's why they shot him?" Elizabeth asks.

Wes raises his eyebrows and lets out a loud *duh*.

"You think cops would've shot him if he was white?"

Instead of answering that, this white boy named Liam says, "He didn't get shot because he was Black. He had that toy gun. The cops probably thought it was real and couldn't tell his age. They maybe shot him to stop him from hurting someone."

"So I'll ask my question differently," Wes says. "If he was white, would cops have talked to him first, or shot him?"

Elizabeth interrupts. "But when did this happen? Because the world's not that way now. And I don't even see race. I just see humans."

"Okay, so maybe you don't see race," Wes tells Elizabeth. "But cops see race. That's why they shoot us or treat us differently than they treat you. So can you help cops see like you? Can you help them see that we're all human? That we humans should all get the same treatment? Or maybe you can become a cop and help change things?"

She shrugs him off, rolling her eyes. "Ugh. Why are we even talking about this?"

Wes shrugs too. "Oh. So you want us to stop talking about this, but you don't actually want to stop this from happening."

Liam tells Wes, "I still think that boy didn't get shot because he was Black."

"Liam, when you look like us"—Wes points at

his own face, then at me and our other Black and Latino friends—"people think we're doing something wrong even when we're not. *That* is why that cop shot him. *That* is why we get treated like we're trouble for no reason."

"Facts, Wes," I say. "This stuff keeps happening."

"True," Devin says. "I don't know how many people know about this kid named Lesandro. But I'm Dominican and he was too. Grown-ups saw him, thought he was trouble, and kicked him out of a store that he ran into for safety. Then he was stabbed to death by a gang. He was fifteen."

Mr. Carrión helps Devin. "His last name was Guzman-Feliz. Lesandro Guzman-Feliz."

Devin thanks Mr. Carrión. "Good lookin' out."

I look at Devin. "He was fifteen?"

"Yeah. Up in the Bronx. He was the wrong guy—innocent—but this gang chased him for blocks. The grown-ups in the store he ran into could've saved his life. Instead, they did what Wes said, what's true—they see us and see trouble."

"Some people are clueless." I roll my shoulders and soft-punch my fist in one hand.

Devin says, "I wonder what would've happened if all of the boys and men in these stories were white."

"They would've been killed too," Liam says.

"Really?" Wes asks. "Then name some who got shot dead."

Liam can't name one.

"Exactly," Wes says, then he starts naming Black victims. "Trayvon Martin . . ."

Devin adds another. "Michael Brown—the teenager from Ferguson."

Erik continues, "The dude that white cop shot in the back while he ran away. In South Carolina?"

"Walter Scott," Mr. Carrión helps.

Elijah names another. "That man who just sat in his car as the white cop unloaded a gun on him. Castle?"

Mr. Carrión says, "Castile. From where that singer Prince was from. Minnesota."

I didn't know Wes, Erik, Devin, and Elijah were up on the news like this.

I check for the whole class's reaction. Most of the white kids are quiet. Mark and Paul are white and look as upset as us. Nancy and Kat are white too and look upset.

Mr. Carrión turns on the overhead projector light, and a picture of Tamir Rice flashes in front of the class. "This is Tamir Rice. You see he's around your age. How would it make you feel if this happened to one of the kids here?"

It goes real quiet.

Me and Dan stare at each other. He eyes me like, *Are you all right?*

I look over at Wes. He also eyes me like, *You okay?*

Nah. I'm not.

Leaving class, me and Wes walk out together. Erik, Devin, and Elijah are right behind us.

Wes tells me, "Some of these kids don't get it. They don't feel it the way we do."

Erik stops and folds his arms. "Bruh, can you believe Elizabeth really said, 'I don't see race'? Wait." His face lights up how faces do when people realize something. "Maybe if she doesn't see race, that's why she doesn't see racism. Like, she wishes we had no problems so there's no problems to fix?"

Wes nods. "That. Is. Deep. If she would've came at us with *just* that, I might have said she's *trying* to help. But she's not, because she said, 'When does that *ever* happen? Never,' when we said cops shoot and kill kids like us."

"She was trying to say we're imagining this stuff," I add.

Devin says, "She wants to stay blind."

Then what hit me earlier hits me again: It's like everyone out here has such different feelings about this. We're in so many different lanes.

First, me and my Black, mixed, and Latino friends are all shook by these shootings.

Second, some of the white kids are seeing this stuff and are upset too.

Third, some white kids like Elizabeth, Brittany, and Liam don't look upset at all and don't want to believe racism is real.

Then I see a bunch of white kids in a whole other lane. They joke and play and laugh and look like they are nowhere close to how me, Wes, Erik, Devin, and Elijah feel. Me, Wes, Erik, Devin, and Elijah should be in that lane, too, where we could just be jokey and not have to worry.

I wish I was in *Into the Spider-Verse* and another universe opened up that me, Wes, Erik, Devin, and Elijah could zap into where foul stuff like what happened to Tamir doesn't happen or where we're bulletproof like Luke Cage.

I'm so glad it's Friday, because I'm so done with today. I just want to go home.

On my way there, Chad's across the street on a corner with his friend Andy. They give me the same look as anytime they see me: It's all hate, maybe wishing I'd disappear. Then Chad's face smirks mad evil. Before? I was done with today. Now I'm done-done.

CHAPTER **23**

MY DAD EYES me from the couch as I walk in and slam our apartment door. "Some people! Ugh!"

"*Some people* who? What happened, Stephen?"

I tell him how in advisory I brought up Tamir Rice and thought it'd make me feel better, but now I feel worse. I tell him what everyone said.

I ask, "How'd some white kids react like they don't care? That girl Elizabeth! Dad, she actually said we're imagining this stuff. Forget her. Forget all of them."

My dad's eyebrows lift to the top of his forehead. "Forget her, huh?"

"Yeah. For. Get. Her."

"She doesn't understand. Maybe she'd see differently if she saw what you saw with her own two eyes. Did she and those classmates see that Black Lives Matter bulletin board you mentioned?"

"Nah, they rushed by it. But they should see it. You can't see that board and not feel it—not want to help. Mr. Carrión should show them."

"Good idea. Tell him. And tell me more. What was on that board?"

"Black and white people. Other people too. Showing racism is unfair."

"So, white kids were allies there. Acting like Dan, right?"

Allies. That's a cool way to describe Dan. I remember learning that word in history class when we talked about the countries that helped us fight in the war. "Yeah, the white kids on that board were like Dan. He gets what I see and feel more now. Especially when his cousin is around. Chad's even worse than ignorant—he's a prejudiced hater. And he's always around lately. Ugh! I turn left; he's there. I turn right; he's there."

"Maybe Dan can help with that. What do you think'll happen if you talk to Dan about it? Maybe he can work on his cousin to get him to change? Instead of just doing what you said before, giving him the 'forget you' treatment?"

"Dan knows Chad's foul to me. He gets mad at him too." Another thought hits me. "I don't know how much Dan can get Chad to change. It might be impossible. Chad's been around me for a while and hasn't changed—he's stayed straight grimy. Sometimes to Dan too."

"Well," my dad says, "a lot of things people thought were impossible have been done. Maybe instead of saying it's impossible, say it's possible—and give it a try."

"Yeah, but if he doesn't listen, maybe the best thing to do is forget Chad."

"Could be, but you'll have tried."

"True. And I'll talk to Mr. Carrión. There are some kids with more sense than Chad who might listen."

CHAPTER 24

DAN ISN'T IN school on Monday morning.

During lunch, I text him from our school's bathroom. **Where u?**

As soon as I slide my cell back in my pocket, it vibrates.

It's him. **Home sick. Flu.**

I can't believe it!

After school, I don't want to hang with Chad, Jen, Jeremiah, and Christopher without Dan. I told Wes I want to chill with him more and I'll try again. So when I see Jen, Jeremiah, and Christopher at different parts of the school day and they talk about linking up after school, I say I can't today.

At dismissal, it happens.

Walking out of school, I see Wes. "I'm thinking about hitting the comic store. You down?"

"With who? Dan and them?"

"Nah. He has the flu. Just me and you."

"The flu? That sucks. I feel bad for him." Wes means it. "My parents made me get a flu shot last year and I still got the flu. Flu sucks."

I wish Dan could see Wes now, saying nice stuff about him.

"Yeah, it sucks. So, the comic store?"

"I'm picking up my little sister from her elementary school. Let me walk her home; then I'll meet you at the comic spot."

"Bet."

We split in different directions.

All of a sudden, I feel less stressed. Because the biggest stress in the store will be choosing which comic to read.

The closer I get to the comic store, the more I get amped. The comic store is the opposite of drama. It'll be just fun.

I notice I'm walking faster.

But when I turn onto the comic store's block, I freeze. Across the street, Chad is on the corner.

I duck behind a truck. When a bus passes between us, I dip into the store.

⇆

The store is extra Halloweeny. Someone OD'd and put a clown mask on the face of the Darth Vader statue as tall as a grown man. On the ceiling, an inflatable Spider-Man swings on a web, chasing an inflatable green-skinned witch on a broom.

I walk aisle to aisle, scanning for a mostly empty spot.

BOOM.

All the way to the left of the store, the aisle with the hardcover graphic novels has *no one* in it. I go in and take my time looking from shelf to shelf. I grab a Miles Morales comic.

"Hey," the comic book store owner greets someone who walks in.

"Hi."

I stiffen. *That sounds like . . .*

I peek through the openings of shelves. It's Chad.

He squints from aisle to aisle like he's searching for someone.

I spy as he gets closer and closer and . . .

. . . Why is he coming toward MY aisle?

I don't have time to jet into another one. I know it's dumb, but I grab a random comic off the shelf, hold it over my face, and hope he won't recognize my back.

It's like forever goes by, but it's more like seconds.

"Stephen."

UGH! I lower my comic, turn around, and front like I didn't know he was here. "Chad. You here."

"Yeah. I saw you come in, so . . ." He pauses. "You alone?"

I lie. "Actually, I was just leaving."

"Hold up." Chad snatches the comic from my hand. "*Black Panther*? Again? Why're you reading trash?"

"I . . ."

"Oh. Because he's Black? I get it." Chad flips the pages like he smells a stinky garbage bag. "What a wack hero. I mean, what king would—?"

A voice pops up in our aisle.

"That's the comic I came for."

Chad turns and his mouth flaps open.

It's Wes.

For me, it's Wes, my boy, showing up.

For Chad, it's Wes, a whole other guy. The Wes who Chad played Hands with back in the day. The Wes who told Chad he'd punch him in the face when Chad OD'd during Hands. The same Wes who said Chad ran away then.

Wes puts his hand out. "Chad, can I see that?"

Chad gives Wes the book without speaking. Then he leaves so fast without saying bye to either of us that he's basically running.

Wes turns to me. "He sounded like he was cutting on you. I told you he'll go too far if you let him."

I nod. "He was dissing Black Panther."

"I bet. Chad's the kinda guy who hates when we're on top or winning. Bet he thinks we oughta be lower than him." Wes looks at the comic. "And who's more on top than Black Panther, y'feel me? He runs a whole country."

I nod, and Wes eyes the door and laughs. "So why you think Chad ran out of here so fast?"

I shrug.

"Because he's a punk, for real."

I give him props. "You remind me of T'Challa. I mean, the Black Panther. You and him have the same boldness."

Wes studies the cover of the *Black Panther* comic. "Is the comic as tight as the movie?" Then he stops talking like he just realized something. "Hold up. This is a teenage Black Panther. He kinda looks like me, right?"

I check. "Dang. This is bananas. This is *you*-you."

Wes loves it. It's cool—his face reminds me of how I feel when I see me in Miles Morales.

"You buying anything?" he asks me.

I shake my head. "I just came to read. I didn't bring money."

"I'll buy this. Let's hit somewhere and read it."

"Word."

"We gotta hang out on the reg like we used to," I tell Wes as we head out of the store.

He huffs a laugh. "That's on you." He joke-pretends to get in a boxer stance to throw a soft jab at me.

On reflex, I throw my hands up, because when me and Dan do this, it's an invite to slap-box. "Oh, you trying to slap-box? C'mon."

He puts his hands down. "Nah. Not here." He lowers his voice so what he says is for us. "We the only Black kids on this block. We can't slap-box in front of these people."

My mind rewinds to when me and Dan slap-boxed close to here and how that white couple reacted. Dang, how Wes can relate to that makes me feel even more that I need to hang with him with no long breaks. "Faaaacts."

CHAPTER 25

I END UP telling Wes I'll walk to school alone tomorrow morning, since Dan has the flu.

"Nah." Wes taps my arm. "Me, Devin, Erik, and Elijah will come for you."

"That's three blocks out the way for you and them."

He shakes his head, waving me off. "Bump that. What time?"

⇆

The next morning, all four of them are in front of my building when I step out.

Seeing them? It's a feeling I can't explain. I haven't rolled-rolled with them for a minute. But does that mean they won't roll with me? Nope.

"Whattup." I step toward them on the curb, realizing my super, Junior, did something he never does for me. Junior held the door open and then stepped out behind me onto the sidewalk. He stands at my building's door, about a car's length from us. At first I think he's being nice to me, but I see how he hovers back there and eyes us. This random thought hits me. Maybe it's not random. *Junior looks at us like he stared down that thief who took his bike.* Another thought comes: *Is he trying to see if one of my friends' faces matches the thief's?*

Then I see something else. Some white people eye us weird, how Junior does.

It's all in your head, Stephen, I think. *Dan told you you were imagining whe—*

Wes leans in to me, loud enough for us to hear, squinting at the white people. "They eye all Black kids who come to your neighborhood like we trouble?"

What? He sees them eyeing us different than the white kids on the street?

I had to point that out to Dan. And even then, Dan didn't see it.

For the whole day, chilling with them is like this. Things I have to point out for my white friends to notice, Wes and them spot instantly. We have some sort of ESP. But instead of extra-sensory perception, I'd call it extra-street perception. It's an X-ray vision about stuff plus a mental telepathy/mind-reading thing we all have with each other. And it feels dope.

Being with my white friends, they get me in some ways. Being with Wes, Devin, Erik, and Elijah, they get me in other ways. But I won't front: During the day, I wish every now and then that both crews would chill together. I think they'd like each other.

So before dismissal on the second day we hang, I ask Wes, Devin, Erik, and Elijah if they'll go to the park with me.

Elijah jumps in. "Wes, let's do it."

Wes nods at me. "Bet. Right after school."

⇆

The first twenty minutes of Wes, Devin, Erik, and Elijah with Jen, Jeremiah, and Christopher is chill. We hang how my mom said I used to play as a toddler—next to other kids in sandlots, but sort of doing my own thing: parallel play. My Black and Latino friends stay in their lane. My white friends in theirs.

But the next half hour, Christopher does something that swerves us all into the same lane, fast-fast and good-good. He yells, "Someone time me climbing that fence!" and rushes to the one that I almost fell from trying to be in his lane.

Devin calls to Christopher, amped, "Hold up. You nice at climbing?"

Christopher points at me. "As good as Miles Morales. Stephen is the new Spider-Man, you know."

"No disrespect, Stephen." Devin's voice is a relaxed fun, the most he's sounded since he's been here. "But I'm Miles."

I tell him, "That's cool."

"C'mon. Let's climb," Devin goes to Christopher, not competitive, just chill.

Something in me makes the next thing come out, fast. I don't know why. "No one time them. Let them just climb for fun."

And Devin and Christopher do. And my white, Black, and Latino friends become one solid group of cheering for them to get up to the top. Well, everyone except Wes.

Wes isn't awkward or obvious, but separate. I notice it and talk to him on the low. "You good?"

"I don't really be around white kids. With everything happening. Not since me and Chad played Hands. But your friends seem cool. I'm just looking, observing." Wes just looks over, smiling. I get it. I get why he wants to make sure my friends are cool.

Jen: "Go, Devin!"

Erik, to me: "What's your man's name again?"

Me: "Christopher."

Erik: "CHRISTOPHER! DEVIN! Go, bro! Go!"

When Christopher and Devin make it to the top—YOoooo, they laugh so hard, you'd think they were friends since diapers. Us standing start laughing too!

That's when I see out of the corner of my eye: Chad.

He stands at the fence outside of the stadium by the parked cars, looking at us. Is he mad? His eyes are tight. Who knows how long he's been watching? Then Chad does what he did before, when he saw Wes. He U-turns and leaves.

⇆

I watch all of my friends while we play. Right now? I feel there's no lane. I want to feel this every day, every minute. Then I look at Wes again. He's in a lane, and he's careful about stepping in ours.

I hear my dad's advice: *You don't want to be in prejudiced people's lanes because that puts you in their hands, and if they have you where they want you, they'll hurt you.*

I wonder if that's what Wes is doing. Not stepping in this lane to make sure they don't play him or hurt him.

My Puerto Rican friend Elijah laughs so hard he's

crying with my white friend Jeremiah, who laughs just as hard.

My Dominican friend Devin and my white friend Christopher sit elbow to elbow, pointing at one cell phone screen, smiling, and finishing each other's sentences.

At one point, Wes comes over and sits side by side with me. "Too bad Dan couldn't be here. If you speak to him, tell him feel better."

Wes means it. When he goes off to practice his handball serves, I text Dan. How r u? Wes just said it b lit if u were here. Says 2 feel bttr.

4 real? Dan texts back.

We go back and forth for a minute; then Dan texts, Bruh, takin a nap. Zapped.

⇆

The next day, it's like this too. Here and there, my friends on this side and my friends on that side swerve out of their normal lanes and into each other's. And it feels good to mix it up and chill together.

Wes is even playing Hands with Christopher and Jeremiah, and they don't OD and smack and try hurting him the way Chad did. Each Hands game Wes plays, he doesn't say it, but I see his face and body language.

He trusts my white friends more and more. He relaxes with them more and more and likes them more.

And Chad? I guess he feels that this really isn't his group anymore, since Dan's not here and Wes and my other boys are. Now Chad's probably back to hanging with Andy and Gabe, and I like that.

CHAPTER **26**

IT'S FINALLY THE Friday before Halloween.

Dan's still sick.

Chad is extra on top of me all day. On the way into school, he smirks at me. At lunch, he comes up to me. "So, my cousin isn't around. You're still coming to my haunted house, right?"

Jen jumps in. "Yes, we're still coming. I need to see this haunted house with my own eyes."

"Cool, then. Be ready to be scared!" Chad points at me and does that Black comedian's joke. "He wasn't ready!"

He leaves.

Why'd he point at me? Maybe it was random. I'm going. It won't be the same without Dan, though.

⇆

Right after dismissal, me, Jen, Jeremiah, and Christopher meet Chad and Gabe in front of the school.

We start walking, and I feel the Halloween vibe everywhere. People carry grocery bags full of candy. Little kids are in costumes from their school parties.

Gabe walks over to me and says, "I'm surprised you're coming."

"Why?"

"Heard you can't handle stuff."

"Who says?"

"Chad used to," Gabe says. "But he said you changed."

I don't say anything, and for the next two blocks, Gabe brags about how creepy they made the haunted house look.

We cut through the park to get to Andy's and pass the handball court. I see Wes far-off, talking to some guys, maybe waiting to play. He turns his head and catches my stare. I raise my hand and nod whattup and he raises a whattup hand back at me. Now I wish he was with us too.

Andy's building is the first one after the park, and we head to the side where a ramp leads to the basement.

To anyone not with us, this ramp is just a ramp to a door to the basement. To me, it feels like a door into the Upside Down world of *Stranger Things* or something. My heart beats faster and harder.

I pull out my cell to text Dan. **At ramp. About 2 go in. Gabe is acting kinda wack tho.**

My phone shows Dan starting to type something. Then he stops. Then he starts typing again. Then he stops.

Chad's voice comes from behind me. "Go in first."

Me? I wonder. *Why me?*

Gabe teases, "Thought Chad said you weren't a scaredy-cat anymore."

Jen, Christopher, and Jeremiah defend me with "He's not scared," and "You should've seen Stephen in the factory," and "If he can handle the factory, he can handle this, *easy*."

From the top of the ramp, I look around me. People everywhere. Little kids are playing tag. Grown-ups sit on benches near the kids. What could happen with so many people out here?

"He's scared," Gabe says again about me.

I touch my bracelet. "Bet I'm not."

CHAPTER **27**

I SLOWLY START down the ramp.

I think to myself, *It's just a door. Open it.*

I reach out and push it open a crack. Then some more and I peek in. Nothing.

I stare harder into the darkness. Nothing moves. No sound.

I step in.

The only light comes from the open door behind me.

Then something in the room moves. I see a shadow of someone about my height. *Who is—?*

The shadow pitches something at me.

BOOM!

Something hits me hard between my eyes, and all I can do is cup my forehead with both hands.

The room spins.

The weird thing is, I don't feel hit. I feel shock. Then wobbly. Then *blood.*

My blood.

I reach out my hand to feel for the door I came through.

"I'm going in!" I hear Christopher run down the ramp, and then he's there at the door.

Jen is with him, yelling, "Oh my god! You're bleeding, Stephen!"

"What?!" Jeremiah rushes over too.

I stumble out into the sunlight and open my eyes again. Blood is on my hands, dripping on my shirt.

Jen grabs me by one side and Christopher grabs my other. They guide me up the ramp.

"I think I'm good," I tell them.

"No, you're not good!" That's Jeremiah's voice.

I hear Gabe and Chad hoot and holler, laughing about what I look like.

"He's like a human unicorn, with a knot between his eyes instead of a horn!" Gabe says.

"I guess the ghosts didn't want him in there!" Chad laughs. "One must've thrown something at him."

Thrown something? Is that what they said? Like they know?

"Just shut up," Jen shouts at Chad and Gabe.

"Yeah," Christopher tells them, "it's not the time to make jokes."

Then a crowd of grown-ups arrives.

"What happened to that boy?" a woman asks.

"Can he see?" a man asks.

"Sheesh!" another man says. "If whatever hit him landed an inch to the left or right, it would've taken his eye out."

I'm kind of spinning when, all of a sudden, Gabe is in my face, taking a photo. He shows Chad. "Look at this shot!"

Jen grabs his phone. "Are you crazy? You're taking pictures when he's hurt and bleeding?! I'm deleting these *now*!"

A shout comes from the direction of the park. "Is that *Stephen*?!"

"Is that Wes?" I ask Jeremiah and Christopher as I blink in the voice's direction.

"Yeah," Christopher says. "He's running over here with a lot of guys! And he looks *mad*-mad."

That's when I hear Wes yell again. "Chad, if you and your friends did this to Stephen, you're getting beat!"

And guess what happens.

Chad and Gabe run. They run away from us so fast, they don't look back.

Wes comes through the crowd to me, takes off one of his shirts, rolls it into a ball, and presses it to my head.

"Ouch!" I wince.

Wes snaps, "Stop flinching away. You need pressure on that."

I notice the Jordan symbol on his shirt. "You using *that* shirt?"

"Look at your face! You bleeding and you care about my shirt?"

His shirt cost a hundred dollars. I know because kids in school talk about wanting that shirt.

I stop moving my head away and let him press it against my knot.

That's when I hear another familiar voice that shocks me. *"What happened?!"*

I ask Wes and everyone, "Is that Dan?"

Wes shouts at Dan, "Your cousin did this and ran! You knew he planned this?"

"No way! I didn't know. I'd never hurt Stephen!"

Dan starts walking over. "Dang, Stephen. Your face."

I tell him, "I thought you were sick. Your parents said not to go out."

"I am. They did. But when you said you were coming here, I got a weird feeling it wasn't right, and I ran out."

Wes asks me, "Where your parents now?"

"Home."

Wes examines my head. "You're bleeding less. I'm taking you there."

Dan grabs my other arm. "Me too."

We walk. On one side of me: Dan, Jen, Christopher, and Jeremiah. On the other side of me: Wes and a bunch of his friends from the handball court. On both sides, everyone talks about what happened to me.

Dan and Wes take turns cracking jokes to cheer me up.

Every time I laugh, I wince. "Y'all need to stop. My head hurts when I laugh."

But they don't. Dan and Wes don't stop trying to cheer me up. They keep telling me I'm lucky that whatever hit me missed my eyes.

And I don't stop thinking how lucky I am that they're my boys.

CHAPTER 28

I STARE AT the ceiling of our kitchen and press an ice pack on my forehead. The cold hurts so bad, I move it away.

Wes grabs the ice pack and presses it on my knot. "Keep it on, for real."

My dad tells me, "It hurts but it helps. You're lucky the cut isn't so deep."

I nod. I'm dumb happy I don't need to go to the hospital for stitches.

"Okay. So what happened?" My parents want to know everything.

I keep it general, like it could've been an accident, leaving it to their imagination that maybe something fell on me or I ran into something. I say where it happened: "In a kid from school's basement." I explain why I went in: "Kids from school made a haunted house down there that I was amped to see."

Saying it all out loud, I sound like a little-little

kid and hate that I was so trusting—wanting to go in a haunted house so bad that I followed heads I knew I shouldn't trust. Ugh.

My parents don't ask for more details. Whew! I speak, they just listen, and it feels good they're not judging me. I don't need more pain on pain.

When I'm done, Mom finally says, "This is terrible. You just wanted to have fun and go into a haunted house. And *this* happened."

My dad starts laughing, and I look at him. It's a laugh that lets out stress. "All because of a haunted house." He chuckles at my mom. "And you worried about our son losing his innocence. Looks like we still have our innocent son."

She smirks back, then busts into a laugh too.

It's good to hear them laugh. The harder they laugh, the better I feel, because I hate stressing them. The more they laugh, the less stupid I feel . . . but I think about that word my dad used: innocent.

Whoever threw something at me could've blinded me. But whoever threw something at me also opened my eyes, and I'm starting to see things that innocent me didn't. Stuff I need to see.

CHAPTER **29**

MY PARENTS FINALLY stop hovering, and me and my friends go to my room.

"Bruh, shut the door?" Wes asks as we walk in my room.

I do, and he steps face-to-face close with Dan. They look in each other's eyes, and without using words, they say a whole lot to each other.

Finally, Wes speaks. "You know *who* I'm thinking about."

"Chad," Dan says.

Wes nods. "And you know *what* I'm thinking."

Dan answers, "It was his idea. He got Andy to throw whatever at Stephen."

"Facts, Andy was missing."

"But why?" Dan asks. "Why Stephen?"

"Because he couldn't do it to me. He likes hurting *us*."

My mind goes to when Wes told me Chad kept hurting him in Hands.

Wes's voice goes so low and forceful that I feel his words more than my bloody, pounding forehead. "Bruh, me and my friends are getting Chad back. Him and his boys' faces are gonna be worse than Stephen's."

Dan stays quiet.

"You can't," I tell Wes.

"Have to," Wes says. "If we don't get even, what's next? Other people think they can hurt you too? Or they trap some other Black kid in the future? Nah."

I trace the bloody letters of WHAT LANE? on my bracelet. I think of lanes. "Wes, going there and beating him up will do what?"

"Make it stop from happening again."

I look at Wes. Yo! *His* face. He reminds me of how my dad looked when we watched the Tamir Rice video and I thought my dad might break his laptop in two with his bare hands. This also reminds me of things me and my dad spoke about.

I look at Dan. "I need you to handle Chad."

Dan puffs up, clenches his hands, and holds his fists up so awkward. "Okay. I'll get Chad and punch his face."

Me and Wes bust out laughing.

Wes snort-chuckles. "Dan, you don't really hold up your hands that way to fight, right?"

I laugh harder. "*Oww!*" I slap my hand to the

knot between my eyes because laughing that hard made it hurt, but smacking it hurt me more.

Wes asks Dan what I wonder. "So you gonna beat up your own cousin?"

Dan puts his fists down. "Who am I kidding? I've never been in a fight. Just slap-boxed with Stephen."

"Dan, you got me wrong. When I say 'handle' him, I don't mean with your fists."

"How, then?" Dan asks me.

"Tell Chad you know what he did and why. And he better fix it, or . . . I don't know what. You just gotta talk with him."

Wes is still amped. "No disrespect, Stephen, but that kumbaya 'talk to Chad' crap is soft. You think it'll change him? You know what'll change him. If we stomp on him. If he gets a foot in his—"

"Then what?" I interrupt Wes. "Why'd you say we couldn't slap-box near the comic store?"

He eyes Dan. His expression says he doesn't want to say in front of him. "You know why."

"Exactly. It's what we spoke about in advisory. Which is why it'd be better if you don't ride that lane. People think that's our lane. That we're violent, or trouble." I turn to Dan. "You know how that white couple almost called the cops on me when we slap-boxed?"

Dan nods.

"And how Junior barked on me like I was a criminal and knew the bike thief? Or that man in the supermarket's bakery?"

"Yeah. All that was messed up."

"So picture Wes and his friends getting caught beating up Chad and two white boys," I say. "What you think'll happen?"

"You're right."

"And Chad getting beat up by Wes won't change how he thinks. It'd probably make him angrier toward us."

"True," Dan breathes out hard. "Whew. I've been thinking a lot about how messed up Chad is. Me and my parents saw what happened in Charlottesville with white supremacists, and how one of them actually drove into a crowd of protesters and killed someone. When I saw your bloody face . . . it made me scared of what Chad could do. Bruh, you think he could do something like that driver in the future?"

I nod. "If Chad keeps riding this lane, who knows."

"Okay," Dan says. "My family has to do something about him. I'll start by talking to them now."

Dan lifts up his fist, and this time it's to fist-bump Wes.

Wes bumps him back. "Yeah, and tell Chad if he doesn't try fixing this, I'll fix his face."

CHAPTER **30**

THAT NIGHT, I stare up at the solar system on my ceiling. I remember my dad telling me, *The world is yours*.

He was right, in a way.

After Dan and Wes left this afternoon, I got texts from Erik, Devin, and Elijah checking in to see how I was. And then Jen and Jeremiah and Christopher texted too.

Because of them, it feels like the world is in my lane. That feels like power. They have my back. And they swerve from different lanes to chill together sometimes. It's cool and I want that to keep on.

I look down at my bracelet's words—WHAT LANE? I don't know how many times I've looked at this thing. Now the words're splattered with blood. As I rub it off, I replay everything up to my getting set up. All of a sudden, what comes to mind is a feeling: *Maybe I need to think deeper about this lane stuff.*

I can't let people use it on me to get me in wrong lanes—to do dares or let them trap and hurt me.

Like Christopher and Dan said, things don't usually end well if we ride in Chad's lane.

And like my dad said: Not everyone who is supposed to be friendly is. I need to wake up more of my white friends so they see prejudice is real. They can fix that in their lane.

Tomorrow's not New Year's—it's Halloween—but I have a new goal: to stop trying to do what everyone does and start really doing me.

I'll swerve into the lanes I choose. Maybe even find new ones.

ACKNOWLEDGMENTS

Thanks is a fraction of my appreciation for my agent, Charlotte Sheedy. Charlotte, you're family in many ways, including how you surround me with those who do what the best of family does. That brings me to more family—Nancy, as my editor, you get what I want to say and you amplify my voice. Thanks to everyone on the Nancy Paulsen team.

Ma, you're everything. To my daughter and wife—thanks for supporting my writing and sharing me with the world. To my sisters, nieces and nephews, and in-laws: we're doing this! To all kids, kids of color, mixed kids, and families who feel there should be no lanes—let's gooooo!

To all of our allies and accomplices. We're jigsaw puzzle pieces that fit into the bigger picture of our whole human family. Thank you to those who unify our world and build greater awareness, empathy, and upliftment.

I grew up in a tough, segregated neighborhood. If you're from Red Hook, Brooklyn, or beyond and helped me be positive when negatives nearly dragged me down, thank you. If you made sure I didn't lower my volume to blend in but helped raise my voice to be better for us all—you're awesome.

I've had WOW experiences and connections with my first and second books—*Secret Saturdays* and *Tight*. Those journeys built me up to build the world of *What Lane?* Thank you if you've fueled me on that course to get here.

Childhood should have spaces where kids can be kids. This book is for everyone creating and protecting those spaces. I'm lucky as an adult to have taught for over twenty years because I've gotten to do that. That's also why I write. This book is about a kid trying to hold on to joy as the world of adults tries to snatch it from him. It is for those of us who are uncomfortable with conversations about people being different. *What Lane?* is for all who raise the volume of kids to do the same and who make sure kids don't relive lives of limit.

Tough topics can be tough. Sometimes it's too tough to connect "eye to eye." This book is for everyone who wants to try—even if it means connecting "shoulder to shoulder" as we walk with young people into better tomorrows.

PRAISE FOR TORREY MALDONADO

TIGHT

- Christopher Award
- *Washington Post* Best Children's Books of 2018
- ALA Notable
- ALA Quick Pick for Reluctant Readers
- CCBC Choices 2019
- ALSC Notable Children's Recordings

"I was riveted by Bryan's journey, breaking down stereotypes and becoming his own kind of superhero. This, in and of itself, is not only Bryan's superpower but Maldonado's as well. Loved this book!"

—JACQUELINE WOODSON,
National Book Award–winning
author of *Brown Girl Dreaming*

"*Tight* hits all the right notes in delivering a suspenseful tale of what it means to become a man in a world split by superhero devotion and macho swagger. A thoughtful look into the pitfalls of male friendship and a riveting addition to tween lit."

—G. NERI, Coretta Scott King Honor–winning
author of *Yummy*

"Looking for a tale of a good kid trying to navigate the dark temptations that can only come from a one-sided friendship? Seek ye no further. This is a book featuring a complexity of character we're lucky to find in a 21st century middle grade novel. Torrey Maldonado hits this one out of the park."

—BETSY BIRD, *A Fuse #8 Production*, *School Library Journal*

★ "[Maldonado] excels at depicting realistic and authentic interactions between middle school boys. An excellent addition to libraries with fans of David Barclay Moore's *The Stars Beneath Our Feet*, Jason Reynolds's *Ghost*, and character-driven realistic fiction."

—*SCHOOL LIBRARY JOURNAL*, starred review

"Through Bryan's believable, emotionally honest first-person narration, Maldonado skillfully shows a boy trying to navigate parental desires and the societal expectations of his Brooklyn neighborhood while trying to figure himself out. Readers will be rooting for Bryan to make the right choices even as they understand the wrong ones."

—*KIRKUS REVIEWS*

"Maldonado's novel quietly interrogates toxic masculinity in a story that will resonate with middle-grade readers who, just like Bryan, are questioning who they are, who they want to be friends with, and how those choices will impact their lives."

—*BOOKLIST*

"The author shrewdly builds suspense, fueling readers' dread that Bryan's poor choices will have dire consequences. . . . This is a psychologically intricate story of the challenges and rewards of family, friendship, and discerning one's true self."

—*PUBLISHERS WEEKLY*

"A book about making good choices and knowing who your real friends are, topics that are relatable to nearly everyone. . . . It is an engaging story and readers will find themselves rooting for Bryan."

—*SCHOOL LIBRARY CONNECTION*

SECRET SATURDAYS

- ALA Quick Pick for Reluctant Readers

"The world these boys live in is all too real. Torrey Maldonado writes with insight and authenticity about friendship and tough choices. It's a story you won't forget."

—COE BOOTH, *Los Angeles Times*
Book Prize–winning author of *Tyrell*

"Torrey Maldonado sticks his finger in an all too familiar hole of a brokenhearted urban community. Playground tough with a sweet center."

—RITA WILLIAMS-GARCIA,
Newbery Honor–winning
author of *One Crazy Summer*

"Ought to be required reading at middle schools everywhere. Maldonado gives us both voice and heart. His young characters navigate a challenging world with endearing earnestness, lively style, and a heartening desire for true dignity."

—E. R. FRANK, award–winning
author of *Life Is Funny*

"Explores inner-city life for a middle school audience with sympathy and humor . . . readers will find both insight and hope."

"Notable for its viscerally authentic treatment of setting . . . infectiously readable, and its characters are sympathetically realized."

"Resonates with the authenticity of a preteen doing his best in an urban landscape that has taught him all he knows."

"A story of friendship, survival, deception and relationships . . . a fast read, entertaining and high interest."